Calamity Canyon

A Work of Historical Fiction

by Bo Mandoe

Based on a True Story

Calamity Canyon
Copyright 2024
by Bo Mandoe
All Rights Reserved
923 Publishing
ISBN: 979-8-9881229-1-3

This book is dedicated to the people
of the southwest, past present and future.

Table of Contents

Dedication iii
Table of Contents v
Foreword vii
Part One 1
Chapter 1: Summer 1993 3
Chapter 2: Summer 1994 21
Chapter 3: Summer 1995 41
Chapter 4: Winter 1995 55
Chapter 5: Summer 1997 67
Chapter 6: Summer 1999 83
Chapter 7: Summer 2002 91
Part Two 99
Chapter 8: Summer 2007 101
Chapter 9: Summer 2012 117
Chapter 10: Summer 2014 127
Chapter 11: Summer 2018 139
Chapter 12: Fall 2023 147
Chapter 13: Winter 2024 159
Afterword 183
Acknowledgements 185

Foreword

I did not grow up in Mogollon and have never spent more than two months in town at a time, and had our eras coincided my presence would almost certainly have caused the subject to turn to the weather amongst the old-timers in The Bloated Goat Saloon.

At the same time, I might be the perfect person to write about the town specifically because I've visited on and off for over thirty years, have seen it change, and may be able to offer a perspective that bridges the gap between resident and visitor, between locals and tourists.

What follows is not an actual history but rather a dramatic re-imagining of this short period in Mogollon's life, as it transitions from ghost town to a tourist destination encouraging nostalgia for the gold rush era even as the town's residents struggle to keep the next wave of miners from exploiting the 100 year old Gila Wilderness, the first National Wilderness in the United States.

CALAMITY CANYON

It's said that truth is stranger than fiction, which may speak more to the demands of a fictional story to reach a satisfying conclusion, to say something with the arc of its narrative; for real life events do not always have neat and simple answers, or we may not be privy to them at the time they happen. In this sense the town of Mogollon is a character as much as anybody, and its people are just as subject to the ineffable forces of humanity and nature that collide in this narrow canyon.

-Bo Mandoe 2024

Part One

Chapter One: Summer 1993

If you're heading west across the United States and you take a left turn in Albuquerque followed by a series of rights and lefts and ups and downs, maybe, just maybe, you'll find yourself in the mining ghost town of Mogollon, on the edge of the Gila National Forest and Wilderness Area.

If you're lucky a business will be open, and if you're even luckier they'll have a public restroom, for while a bear might poop in the woods your kids probably aren't so adept at it, and in any case there's nowhere to wash your hands besides Silver Creek – and if you think the locals aren't going to notice you sending your kids into the woods and directing them to the creek to clean themselves off, you're probably not going to make it very long in the rugged Southwest.

My name is Frederic Thomsen Fredericksen and I first came to Mogollon when I was seventeen years old.

It was the summer between my junior and senior years of high school, and though I didn't know it then it was to be the first of thirteen trips I'd take to Mogollon over the next 31 years.

My sister Astrid and I were born and raised on the island of Maui, which did not have a four-year college back in the 1990s. In order to get the kind of education you needed to get a job that paid well enough to live on the island, you had to leave the island. It was the kind of paradox that made me suspicious of our entire economic structure. People had been living there for hundreds of years before white men showed up and changed the economy – not to mention the ecology – and now you needed a fancy degree just to afford the cost of living? What about the locals who never got to road trip across the mainland to visit colleges? Who never got a degree at all?

My parents and I flew into Los Angeles (Astrid was attending college in Oregon and had elected to stay over the summer) to visit my mom's parents, then borrowed their Buick Century and set out across California and Arizona, the interstate stretching before us like an event horizon. We camped in State Parks whose names I've blocked from memory, so lacking was their charm. We visited colleges in Tucson and Phoenix and Flagstaff before heading north into Colorado.

It was all a little overwhelming. I was supposed to be gathering information about these schools and their programs in order to make the most important decision of my life, but none of it felt real. Maybe if we'd flown from city to city and I'd only seen the campuses it would've been different; maybe I wouldn't have realized how much I was missing. But the mainland was big, enormously big.

Not only had I grown up on the most remote location on the planet – on an island you could drive around in a day and still get home in time for dinner – I'd spent most of it in school. All I had was a classroom understanding of anything beyond the ocean. For the very first time I was realizing how much more there was to the world than what I knew, and that there must also be more to life outside of the classroom than I'd ever imagined. How was I supposed to choose my life's path on incomplete information?

For that matter, if the world was so big, why was I working so hard to get back to Maui?

It all came out one night at the Morefield campground outside of Mesa Verde National Monument. Mother wanted to spend a day sightseeing but father insisted we stick to the schedule. We had four more colleges to visit between Durango and Denver, then had to backtrack all the way to Los Angeles in just over two weeks.

"Maybe Fred's already seen a school he likes," mother suggested. Their eyes turned to me.

I could feel the pressure of their stares. Somehow I'd become the decisive vote. My next words would determine the trajectory of our trip, and quite possibly my future. But what did I really want?

"I heard Microsoft is offering entry level internships," I said, shrugging my shoulders noncommittally. "Other companies too. It's minimum wage but if you get in on the ground floor…"

I let the implications lie. The truth was, I didn't really know what the implications were. It was something I'd read in a tech magazine. It had painted this image of young people like myself working together in a utopian dream scenario, a community of rising tech moguls building a digital infrastructure for the computers of the future.

"An internship," father said, his tone anything but utopian or dreamy.

"A paying job," I reiterated, "with room for advancement. And good experience! I could take that internship and turn it into any kind of job in the tech industry."

"But why would they hire you over someone with a degree?"

"Nobody with a degree would work for that little," mother put in.

"The cutting edge stuff isn't in schools," I said, pushing the point, "it's at Microsoft and companies like it. One year there and I'd know more than I would learn in four years at a place like these." I waved vaguely to indicate the schools we'd been visiting.

Father mulled over the information. "All the tech companies are on the west coast."

"Sounds like there's time to sightsee after all!" mother crowed.

#

Some two days later and several hundred miles to the south, we abandoned the high desert to navigate the foothills of the Gila National Forest. There was a ghost town in the mountains some snickering locals in Pie Town had encouraged us to visit, and despite their obvious delight in sending us up a lonely mountain road, my parents decided to risk the trip.

Around the five mile marker Bursum Road narrowed and pitched steeply upwards. On the right the hillside leaned toward us until it became a sheer cliff, and on the left it dropped away in dramatic fashion. Suddenly we were winding along the side of a mountain on a road barely larger than the width of the Buick itself. This stretch of terror culminated in a blind turn for which I was glad we had the inside lane, if one could call it such. Anybody coming down the mountain would have been forced toward the edge while we hugged the cliffside, much as I was hugging the door handle.

Father honked the Buick's horn. We rounded the corner safely and the road abandoned the cliff to enter into the heart of the mountain. Then the radiator overheated.

It was a familiar feeling standing by the roadside waiting for the car to cool. We'd owned many a beater over the years, and Bursum road had some similarities to the Haleakala Highway. It was long and windy and slow, and the high elevation made my nose bleed.

A battered old Datsun pickup, the first vehicle we'd seen since turning up Bursum, came to a rolling stop in the middle of the road. Its occupant, a woman in her mid-30's with a deep tan and bright orange hair, leaned over to roll down the passenger window. "Y'all going to *M'Gollum*?" she drawled, a twinkle in her brilliant blue eyes.

"Er, ah, yes," father said, taken aback by the woman's demeanor.

"Is there anywhere to camp?" mother asked, putting an arm around father.

The woman eyed the overheating Buick. "Name's Reese," she said, "Reese Bradley. Tell you what. When your car's up to it, come on into town and stop by The Tilted Windmill. It's my husband's tavern. I'll call around and find you a place to stay."

"You don't have to do that-" father began.

"Thank you very much," mother said, cutting him off. "That's very kind of you."

Reese put a hand to her head, tilting an imaginary hat. Then she drove up the road. Half an hour later, we followed.

We crested the hilltop around the 8 mile marker and began the descent into Silver Creek Canyon. The mountains stretched to the horizon in every direction except behind us, where they gave way to the high desert plains. Across the nearest canyon a gigantic pile of bleached sand popped amongst the faded greenery of the scrub forest: tailings from an old mine, the parts left behind after the extraction process. As we dipped into the canyon more signs from the mining days appeared; the stone framing from an old powder house, where dynamite was stored; steel gates over yawning holes in the hillsides; rusting relics of vehicles and machinery.

Then we rounded the final curve and entered the town of Mogollon itself. It was about the length of a football field. Brick storefronts lined the street like an old Dutch village, or my imagination of one. Most were boarded over. There was a novelty shop that looked like it might open at times. A creek ran down the length of the town, spanned by bridges to access buildings on the far side. One of these sported a classic western façade and a wooden carving of a tilting windmill above the front door.

In the middle of town the creek switched sides with the road. A one-lane bridge that looked like it'd survived since the town's inception gave access to the other side of the canyon. Here the buildings were spaced further apart, miners' cabins and the Old Kelly Store and the Mogollon Theatre and an historic building that used to be a saloon.

I wandered about while my parents went into the tavern. I was more than ready to be out of the car and very excited at the prospect of a comfortable house with the normal amenities of civilized life: hot shower, toilet, television.

The place Reese found for us had all of these… sort of.

The house belonged to Robert Maldonado, a 78 year old cattle rancher born and raised outside of Flagstaff. He'd fallen in love with an extra on the set of a Western film. His newlywed wife Hazel had brought him back to her hometown of Mogollon where they'd raised three kids, all of whom had returned to Flagstaff just as soon as they were able. Hazel had passed away last year, and Robert was currently on an extended visit with his eldest. We were welcome to stay in his house for the rest of our trip if we wanted – so long as we observed his water protocol.

As I was soon to learn up close and more personally than I would have liked, showers and toilets shared two key requirements: water, and a place for the waste to drain. Robert's house, built in 1908, featured a hand-dug stone-lined well in the earthen basement, which ran dry in droughts. Water was accessed through the hand crank in the upstairs kitchen or by turning on an electric pump to feed the downstairs bathroom, which did have a propane water heater, which also had to be turned on before use. Because there wasn't constant water pressure in the line, which the ancient pump couldn't handle, each step had to be done in specific order before taking a hot shower.

And then, as Reese was clear to inform us, we were to use the water for as short a time as possible. As in, turn it on to get wet, turn it off while soaping up, then turn it on again to rinse off. This was to conserve water, but it was also to preserve space in the septic tank. There was no leach field for the house's innocuous wastewater: everything that went down the drain had to be sucked out at a premium cost by a honey bucket company.

"It's like this all the time?" I remember asking. "How did they live this way?"

That was when Reese showed us the outhouse.

Robert Maldonado's house

There were some perks, though. Robert Maldonado had a gigantic satellite dish and a twenty-something inch color television! These quickly became my safe haven.

I'd never had more than five channels available, and PBS stopped counting around the time puberty hit. Suddenly there were several hundred at my fingertips. You had to direct the dish to a certain physical setting in order to connect to each available satellite, which would then broadcast any number of channels. It took several minutes to change satellites, and you could actually see the dish moving in the yard.

Many channels required a subscription. Even more were in foreign languages, or played nonstop advertisements. But there was enough to keep me busy for hours, finding the good satellites and writing down the channels.

And then the strangest thing happened. At one point when I was all by myself in the living room, I accidentally sat on the remote control and lost the picture. Like, the TV went to static and nothing I did could bring it back.

I was distraught. I was in tears. I went running to mother and told her what happened. She tried to help but to no avail: the entire system had been fried by my rear end. And to add insult to injury, father had a hard time believing I was telling the truth.

Eventually he called Robert Maldonado and got the number of a television repair man in Silver City, some seventy miles away. This man had helped Robert set up his system and after a fruitless phone conversation offered to make a house call for a hundred and seventy-five dollars at his next availability… in a week or so.

I had no choice but to do something else.

CALAMITY CANYON

There were actually five kids in this miniature town of 25 people, all quite a bit younger than me, except Felipe and Denny.

Felipe's parents ran a store out of the old Mogollon Theatre, sort of an antique store slash museum; many of the things on the shelves didn't have prices or any possible use except as mining memorabilia or decorative doorstops. I bought a candy bar and a postcard.

Sofia Rosa, the cashier and Felipe's mother, hollered for him in a string of rapid Spanish as she took my money. A sullen looking boy came out from the back of the store. He was short and heavyset and dragged a broom behind him like a shackle. But when his mom told him to show me around he brightened up. And dropped the broom.

Felipe had a Commodore 64, almost as old as the town itself from a technological point of view. We played Wheel of Fortune until it was obvious I knew more about the English language than him. He wanted to move back to Tombstone where his mother was from, but he'd gotten into trouble for setting off fireworks and starting a fire.

That's why they'd moved up to Mogollon, to keep him out of trouble. All he did was work in the store and chop wood.

I wanted to go exploring, but Felipe wasn't into hiking.

Denny was another story. His parents had both grown up in the valley, that is, along the high plains corridor that ran below the Mogollon mountain range; they'd met in high school and had been together ever since. Denny hadn't actually been born in Mogollon, of course, because there wasn't a hospital, but he'd spent his entire life there. Once he'd finished his morning chores he was more than happy to ramble off the trail with me.

I almost stepped on a rattlesnake jumping over the creek. It slithered under a rock but Denny insisted we scare it out. It was too close to town, he said, or we could get paid good money for its skin, I don't remember. I was in a strange place having a strange experience and I just went with it. I rustled at the hole with a long stick. The snake rattled at me angrily. I bothered it some more. It stuck its head out. Denny swung his machete and the snake thrashed in agony. He swung again and it stopped moving.

We carried its body through town slung over the stick. A small crowd gathered to watch Denny skin the snake and roll up its beautiful diamondback and set it into a jar filled with radiator coolant he'd acquired from somewhere to cure.

I don't know what he did with the body.

#

The day before we left Mogollon, the television repair man finally made it to town. His name was Horace Bursum. He was dressed like a cowboy and had a drawl to match.

"I 'member this place," he said, fiddling with the remote, "them old folks kick the bucket? I'd a mind to move up here myself." Horace was well into his sixties.

"I thought maybe you were from the area," father said congenially, "Horace Bursum, Bursum road."

"Naw, that's my great-uncle's side of the family. We don't much talk. What'd you do to this anyway? All my programming's gone."

"Sat on it," I said.

Horace looked at me in surprise. "Ya *what*?"

"I sat on the remote," I repeated, refusing to meet father's eyes. "It was an accident."

"Well, I'm gonna have to do it all over," he said. Then he spent three hours working on the system, reprogramming it from scratch. When he was finally done he scratched his head. "I got no idea what went wrong. Try not to sit on it, I don't want to come up here again unless I'm staying." He took a final look around the house. "A guy could do a lot with this place."

The next day it was finally our time to leave, and I made a big deal out of my relief. Back to the land of convenience and technology, where you could sit down without concern… on the couch or on the throne.

We arrived home to a message on the answering machine. It was Reese Bradley. "Guess what?" her voice bubbled through the static, "Robert Maldonado just decided to sell his house!"

Chapter Two:
Summer 1994

The following summer I graduated from high school and left Maui for a minimum wage tech internship in Seattle. My friend Nick Jensen, who'd graduated the year before, was transferring from USC to the University of Washington to live near his grandfather and had suggested we take a road trip on the way north, in a roundabout fashion, and visit the Grand Canyon. Only knowing of one place in the Southwest I insisted we add Mogollon to our itinerary.

And so we headed east from Los Angeles, making the trip in two days and one night in my grandparents' borrowed Buick Century, whose ever dependable radiator overheated halfway up Bursum road once again. We stopped at The Tilted Windmill to obtain a house key and Kinny invited us over for dinner.

At Robert's- no, at my parents' house, I proudly demonstrated how to turn on the well pump and water heater, let Nick marvel at the actual hand pump in the kitchen, and sat down to show off the range of the satellite dish. But Nick insisted we hadn't driven this far to sit in front of a television. So we walked the length of the town as tourists do, marveling at the rusting mine cars and the blocked off doorways into the stone mountainside, the original cold storage system. During its heyday enterprising residents would saw frozen ice from further up the mountain into blocks and bring it to town to sell; covered in sawdust and stored in the mountain caves it kept produce cool all summer.

Two businesses were open this year in addition to the old theater store. The novelty shop sold birdhouses and model airplanes. Nick tried to engage the owners, two frail men in button down sweaters, in small talk, but all he got were grunts and shrugs.

In the middle of the hot summer day smoke poured from the chimney of a small house surrounded by a yardful of figurines and art sculptures and partially chopped logs.

A sign read 'Mogollon's Mesmerizing Mystical Mirror: hypnotism and readings $5.00." While we stared a woman emerged from the house to gather an armful of firewood. She must've been in her 60s. She wore a bikini top and a flowing sarong around her waist and Birkenstocks. When she saw us staring she smiled. "The house is cold," she explained, "I keep the fire going so I don't have to wear clothes."

I showed Nick the 1968 International Harvester that Robert Maldonado had left behind with the house; not that different from the rusting relics that decorated the town, but supposedly still able to make it from one end to the other. I showed him where Denny and I had fought the rattlesnake. We found openings into the mountain, some with train tracks and others clearly ventilation shafts for the miners. These tended to be vertical and partially hidden by the slope. As alluring as these gaping pits into the very center of the earth were, I'd read enough Tom Sawyer to quell the temptation to venture inside.

CALAMITY CANYON

1968 International Harvester

Anyway, Nick wanted to climb. Just to the west of town stood a modest sized peak boasting an impressive rock outcropping; the view of town would be superb from its vantage point.

By the time we reached the top it was late afternoon and storm clouds had rolled down the mountain to obscure our Kodak moment. We could still see the town, though. Kinny was standing in his yard waving at us. We stood on the very top of the outcropping and raised our arms to wave back.

Then a lightning bolt flashed among the clouds and a crack of thunder split the sky! The spell broke. We looked at each other, simultaneously realizing that Kinny was waving us off the mountaintop.

That night Reese regaled us with local gossip while Kinny nodded stoically at her soliloquy, inserting clarifying details when the opportunity presented itself.

Reese was a fire spotter. Born and raised some seventy miles away in Silver City, she'd earned a forestry degree at Western New Mexico University and parlayed that into a job as one of Bear Wallow's fire lookouts. Two weeks alone on top of a mountain and two weeks off from mid-April through October, with unemployment over the winter. It wasn't a bad gig. She'd been doing it nearly twenty years now.

Kinny ran the tavern during tourist season, approximately the same months. He was as stoic as she was gregarious, polar opposite personalities seemingly ill-suited for their jobs but possibly having developed because of them. Kinny, aka Kindred Spirit, an imposing man with a long braid in his sun-bleached hair, had moved to Mogollon in the early 1980's as part of a wave of hippies seeking to build the utopia they'd envisioned during their long strange trips on the magical mystery tour.

They were in a bit of a feud with a neighbor. Kinny liked to play NPR while he worked around his yard, but the neighbor must've disagreed with his political alignment. He'd mounted a radio antenna halfway up the canyon wall and broadcast recordings of Art Bell at a very similar frequency; the interference made NPR unlistenable. As this wasn't their first clash, Kinny didn't bother trying to reason with him. Instead he called the FCC and reported it. The pirate station was shut down within a week.

Another time, Reese had forgotten her keys in the door of her car. She went out to retrieve them to discover the neighbor had laid possession to the key ring, was in fact swinging it in his fingers and gloating as she passed by. When she demanded the keys back he went into his house and locked the door. So she called the county sheriff, who made the hour plus drive up to town, and they confronted the neighbor. He immediately handed the key ring over to the sheriff.

Every single key had been ground flat. They were all useless. When asked why he'd destroyed the keys, the neighbor said he didn't want to be accused of having used them to steal things.

"It takes all kinds," Reese said, laughing at her own story. "One day a stranger in a cowboy hat came into the tavern, looked around, and announced that he owned the property. My Kinny just stared him down and calmly said, *okay*. Eventually the man left. Then he walked into the novelty shop and did the same thing! The brother working the counter made the mistake of arguing. The stranger said he had documents to prove his claim. The brother threatened to take him to court. The stranger agreed. They would meet at sunrise three weeks hence, armed with lawyers and supporting evidence. It was a modern day duel!"

Reese laughed again. "Some months later that same stranger came back to the tavern, rubbing his hands in glee. He'd lost the case, of course. But it cost the defendant over $7000 in legal fees!"

"Some people just want to fight," Kinny observed stoically.

#

Nick and I found ourselves in one the very next day. It started when I suggested we take the day to recuperate before doing more driving. It was ten in the morning and I'd gotten as far as making a bowl of oatmeal and sitting down to eat it. He'd washed and dressed and packed his bags and was sitting across from me, arms folded, one leg impatiently rocking on the creaky old floor.

"I swear, Fred," he said, "you're the laziest traveler I've ever met. Here we are on the edge of the Gila Wilderness, we could go to the Cliff Dwellings or the Catwalk Park or drive up the mountain to Willow Lake; there's any number of tourist attractions available and you just want to sit here."

"We're in the middle of an attraction," I pointed out.

"You don't even want to go for a hike?"

I shrugged. "I don't really like hiking. I *do* like being in places you have to hike to get to, but here all it takes is going out to the porch and the view's just as good."

Nick bunched up his face muscles in disdain. "I guess I shouldn't be surprised, you were like this in high school. You never commit to anything. You just kind of exist on the periphery."

"Hell you talking about?" I growled, but the words struck deep. I'd floated through every school assignment I'd been given, always doing the minimum necessary to keep my teachers happy. I'd never joined extracurricular activities. It was one path of least resistance after another, even the decision to abandon college for a low-paying entry level position, a decision whose unintended side effect had led to the purchase of the house we were sitting in now. Maybe that was why I'd insisted we come, and was hesitant to leave now that we'd arrived. In some odd karmic way my lack of commitment had led me here, and perhaps it had more to say.

"This place is fascinating," Nick was saying, "there's so much history to learn: how did it get its name? Who found gold in the first place? How did they build the road, for God's sake? If you're not up for anything I'll walk around and talk to people, try to learn what I can. But you're the one with the house here."

"Fine," I said, sighing in exaggerated exasperation, "we'll go for a hike."

Above town the road forked: right to Willow Lake and left to the Fannie Hill Mine and the town cemetery.

"That's more like it!" Nick crowed. "No better place to learn about a town than its cemetery."

The road wound up the north side of the canyon in a series of switchbacks, providing a bird's eye view of the town, the summer sun stretching nearly into the creek itself. We passed several houses as well as decaying cabins, sun-scorched structures of old-growth and corrugated roofing, before the road angled up a creek bed and beyond house and home. Still, here was evidence of mining: holes in the side of the canyon, rock walled terraces, mangled metal remains.

"How many people lived here?" Nick wondered.

We came to another fork: left to the mine, right to the cemetery. We kept walking.

The cemetery was marked with a token fence that may have kept out cattle, but deer and other forest fauna had clearly not been deterred. Neither had the pervasive cacti undergrowth nor the juniper and piñon trees that blanketed the area: in short, the cemetery was entirely overgrown to the point of not being a cemetery so much as a part of the forest that happened to have gravestones dispersed at random amongst the trees. It was so large that, once you passed through the wrought iron gate, you immediately forgot you were fenced into a specific part of the landscape.

And the gravestones! Here was an entire family. Here were influenza babies. Here lay but few older than fifty years of age, and even fewer more recent. Some were no more than metal crosses stuck in the ground. A few were fenced in their own right, tomb-sized stones engraved with poems or scripture. Everything was very Catholic.

There was no Maldonado to be found, nor Mogollon.

"So much for learning about the town."

Nick shot me a look. "I learned a lot. To have a cemetery this big the town must've been a couple thousand people at least. Mostly late 1800's to the 1940's. Do you notice anything about the names?"

I turned away, ostensibly to look at names on gravestones, but when it was safe I scowled. What was he seeing that I'd missed?

"No Asian names," Nick said. "Only Hispanic and Anglo."

"You don't think there were Asians here?" I asked, my back still to him.

"Not buried here."

I didn't get it. I turned to demand an explanation.

"Hey!" A horn honked, causing me to jump. "Give a guy a hand?"

Nick and I turned toward the sound. On the other side of the fence, in the middle of the road we'd walked up, an aging Jeep idled. An old man leaned out the window, holding a bouquet of flowers.

"I'm no spring chicken anymore," the man explained as we walked over. He was bald, with several dark spots on his scalp. He wore a pair of horn-rimmed glasses and a hearing aid. The Jeep, which sputtered out fumes as we spoke, had a hard shell patched with duct tape and a matte black paint job under several years' worth of mountain dust. "It's my wife's birthday."

"What's her name?" Nick said, gesturing at the flowers. "We'd be honored to deliver those."

"Thelma Rozier," the man said, handing over the bouquet. "She's up near the top of the lot. And I thank you kindly."

"It's no problem," said Nick. "Come on."

I followed him back into the cemetery. We found her gravestone easily; it was indeed near the top of the lot, one of several Roziers buried in a row. And next to Thelma's was an empty spot.

I shivered as Nick laid the flowers next to her grave. "Weird to know where your body is ending up."

He gave me an exasperated look. "Come on, let's catch a ride down the hill."

"Now you're talking my language!"

Nick just shook his head.

Then he shook down Mr. Rozier for all the information he could get out of him. The town of Mogollon was named after Juan Ignacio Flores Mogollon, an Official in the Spanish Army and the 36th Governor of New Mexico (from 1712-1715).

Mr. Rozier spat out the window. "He was removed from office for embezzlement. And yet he gets a town, a mountain range, an entire prehistoric people named after him!"

"So the town wasn't here in the 1700s?" Nick asked.

"No," Mr. Rozier said, "not until the late 1800s, after James Cooney found gold. There was a town named after him, ha!" He spat out the window again. "Apaches did for Cooney and a flood did for his town. It never got built up again though."

"Wait, Mogollon flooded?"

"Flooded, burnt, flu epidemic. What hasn't happened here?"

"You weren't alive then though."

"No?" Mr. Rozier laughed, a grating sound. "Kid, I remember the first carriage to drive into this town without a horse in front of it. I remember when they were hauling so much silver out of here it had to be guarded by an entire regiment. And I remember the day it ended." The look that crossed his face was less melancholy than confused. "June 18th, 1942. The mine shut down and overnight, it seemed, everybody moved on. Thousands of people, off to mines in Clifton or Morenci or Douglas, or back east or wherever they came from in the first place. But some of us were born here."

"Did Asian people live here?" Nick asked, glancing my way.

"Orientals?" Rozier said. "Sure, they were here. Hard workers. They had their own cat house and everything, up Coffee Gulch."

"Why aren't any in the graveyard?"

"Not Christian," Rozier said, shaking his head. He spat out the window. "Shouldn't matter, you ask me."

"My parents bought Hazel Maldonado's house," I said, seeing a chance to contribute to the conversation.

"Ah, Hollywood Hazel," Mr. Rozier sighed. "She was too big for this town. I loved her, you know. But then everybody did. Still, if she hadn't come back with that rancher I would've married her first chance I got."

"You didn't get along with Robert?"

"He was fine." Mr. Rozier waved it off. "Never quite found his place here though. Can't raise cattle in the mountains. He got fired from the Forest Service, from the Postal Service, from the Department of Transportation. They mostly lived on her acting money. She ran a gallery for a while in the 60s."

"What did you do, Mr. Rozier?" Nick asked politely.

"Lenny, call me Lenny. I *did* ham radio, and I've never stopped doing it!"

"I'm sorry," said Nick, chagrined. He looked out the window meaningfully. We were nearing the bottom of the canyon. "But there can't be much line of sight out here, can there?"

Lenny frowned. "You never heard of repeaters? The moon bounce? Kid, there's stuff out here you've never dreamed of, things you'll never learn about in your fancy universities. I've seen purple lights float through this valley at night, unearthly purple lights that moved in ways lights shouldn't move. I've heard voices bouncing off the moon that weren't from this planet, non-human voices. And other things too."

"Well, it looks like this is our stop," Nick said. "Thanks for the ride."

Lenny Rozier pulled over and let us out. "My cabin's up the road a ways. Stop by for coffee sometime. I don't get out much anymore."

The moment he drove off Nick and I turned on each other.

"What was that?" I said. "You pump him for information and then shut him up the moment you don't like what you're hearing?"

"You're darn right!" Nick exclaimed. "I don't like what I'm hearing now! The guy was clearly daft. We can't trust anything he said!"

"Your problem is you only see how things are useful to yourself."

"Your problem is you don't know what is."

"That doesn't even make sense!"

"It's what I've been saying all along," Nick pressed. "You don't commit to anything because you don't know what matters to you. You're just out here larping through life!"

I bit off my retort. Nothing I could think to say would make things better. Or change the fact that he was right.

"Look," he said, his voice a tone calmer, "that guy just gave us a treasure trove of information about this town.

You're the one with a house here; if I were you I'd write it down. You never know what might be useful."

I shrugged him off. My memory was good. Besides, hadn't he just said we couldn't trust Lenny? "Didn't you say he was daft?"

"Well sure," Nick grinned, "but it makes a good story!"

Chapter Three: Summer 1995

Home might be where the heart is, but with both of their kids on the mainland my parents' hearts were no longer in Hawaii, so they sold our childhood home and moved to Mogollon, purchasing the nicest vehicle the family had ever owned along the way: a 1984 Toyota Forerunner with 4wd, power windows, and an actual sunroof that tilted open at an angle for ventilation.

In June my internship ended and the tech company – not Microsoft – deigned to offer me further employment, so I was briefly at a loss for what to do next. When I heard that my uncle Erik, the youngest of father's five siblings, was coming to visit from Denmark with his family, including two sons, I decided to attend the reunion.

Father's name is Thom Hansen Fredericksen, or Thom Hans's son Frederic's son. He'd intended to name me Frederic Thomsen Hansen after his grandfather but hadn't understood American law.

Thom's father's name was Hans Fredericksen Thomsen. His father's name was Frederic Thomsen Hansen, and *his* father's name was Thom Hansen Fredericksen. You were your father's and your grandfather's son. This system had worked perfectly fine for countless generations, but when father – Thom – emigrated to America in 1970 after meeting and marrying my mother, Clara Lynn, his surname was frozen. And so I became Frederic Thomsen Fredericksen.

Please call me Fred. Most people do.

Uncle Erik's boys were several years younger than me and spoke little to no English. The older one, Claus, was a huge fan of American basketball. He wore an Olajuwon jersey and a '94 Rockets cap and his Danish was peppered with basketball terms and players names. The younger son, Lars, was still pretty much tied to his mother.

Felipe and Denny were no longer in town. They'd gone down to the recruitment center and enlisted the day Felipe, who was some months younger, turned eighteen. The theatre store was closed, his parents back in

Tombstone. The hypnotist had left town as well, though that had less effect on my summer social scene.

In short, I was still at a loss. After a week of family outings to tourist attractions such as the much-hyped Catwalk Park (a rickety wooden pathway suspended along a sheer canyon) and the old Mogollon cemetery, I was more than jaded with the sleepy ghost town mountain life. Even the satellite system had lost its appeal.

I thought about what Nick Jensen had said. What was there to commit to here? I could walk up the road and visit Lenny Rozier, that would eat up a couple of hours. Then what?

And then one day two girls showed up in town. Their names were Micah and Marisa and they were third year college students spending the summer traipsing about the country. Kinny hired them to paint the exterior of his building, and when it became obvious that I was going to hang around wherever the girls were, he hired me as well.

"Here's the deal," Kinny said on the first morning we showed up to work, "this building is registered as an historic site. It's one of the last standing original buildings in town. The same mason that built your house," he nodded in my direction, "worked on it. What this means is we can't change anything. Not the windows, not the roof, not the walls. Everything has to be redone exactly the way it always has been."

I took a closer look at The Tilted Windmill for the first time. The walls were plaster, much like my parents' house, though more of a sour yellow tone than our off-white color. Sun-scorched wood trimmed out the door and windows, of which there were many. Here and there odd metal bolts protruded from the wall, serving no obvious purpose. The squared-off façade on the front stretched beyond the height of the second floor, looming ominously above the creek bed below.

"How are we gonna paint up there?" I asked.

"Scaffolding," said Marisa. She'd wrapped her sandy brown hair in a bandanna. Freckled, firm features graced her face and her stance exuded competence. She wore work boots and paint-stained overalls and a sleeveless top.

"One side at a time," said Kinny. "We'll do the west wall first. Today we'll set up the scaffolding and start taping the windows. The trim wasn't painted originally so I can't ever paint it." He sighed. "I have to replace the wood every ten years."

"You don't think we'll actually get to painting today?" I asked. "I thought we'd be rolling color already!" I looked around pointedly. There wasn't a bucket of paint to be seen.

Micah chuckled. "Prep takes longer than application."

I tried to focus on the meaning of her words but got distracted by the lips they'd emerged from. She wasn't wearing makeup, neither of them were, but nevertheless her lips sparkled in the morning sun like a reflection in moving water. I was drawn to them as a sailor to mermaids, as rats to the Pied Piper. I barely noticed her waist long jet-black hair or the multiple studs in her ears or the subtle contours of her body.

"We're going to be spraying," Kinny explained. "Well, Marisa will probably be doing the spraying. You and Micah will be there to assist and back-roll."

"Just follow my lead," said Micah. "There's a rhythm to it."

There certainly was. Retrieve scaffolding, hold in place, set together, retrieve more, pass it up, hold in place, set together, secure structure to odd metal bolts whose purpose was finally explained. After a couple of hours the entire west side of the building was accessible through a three-story edifice of steel framing and wooden planked walkways.

Taping off the window trim required a calm and patient eye that I'd not yet developed. After redoing several of my attempts, Micah instructed me to hold the plastic sheeting while she ran the tape. From that point on my job was basically to stand there and, every once in a while, roll out a couple feet of plastic.

Tourists wandered into town as the day wore on. More than one took pictures of us on the scaffolding. It amused me to think that they thought we were locals. After all, how would a tourist know who was from here and who wasn't? For all they knew my Danish relatives lived there too.

Seeing myself through the eyes of a tourist gave me a momentary sense of internal vertigo, as if I'd suddenly changed places with an actual local, someone like Denny or Felipe who'd grown up here. For a fleeting second I felt like I was part of something bigger than myself. Like I'd ceased to exist on the periphery and had actually joined something.

"Good work," Kinny said after lunch, a simple fare of peanut butter and jelly on homemade sourdough served in the side yard. "That's it for today; I'll be opening in a couple hours and can't have minors on site."

"When will we start painting?" I wanted to know.

"Soon enough," he smiled. "There's no rush. You probably won't be here to see the job through. Just stay focused in the moment."

One day he announced a break in the routine: instead of working we were going up to Bear Wallow to visit Reese at her fire lookout and hunt for wild mushrooms. We drove two cars up the bumpy mountain road: Kinny, my parents, and uncle in one (the boys and their mom had stayed home to watch game 4 of the NBA finals); and myself and the girls in the other.

By this point we'd gotten to know each other fairly well. They were grunge heads from outside of Seattle. They knew the company I'd worked for and all the places I liked to go. To say I was infatuated would be putting it mildly.

We spent an hour at the lookout itself, waiting for a break in Reese's requisite monologue to excuse ourselves to go on the actual hunt. Two weeks in a forty-foot tower on top of a lonely mountain could have that effect on anyone, I guessed. She pointed out a cluster of tree stumps around the lookout. "Bob did that," she informed me, "and got fired for it."

Then the mushroom hunt began. We waded into the forest like bears, the crunch of our footsteps telegraphing our presence ahead of us. We were nearly 9000 feet above sea level. Here the trees were taller and straighter than at the cemetery: more alpine, with less cactus undergrowth. Still, everything was very dry.

"It's too dry," Kinny said, echoing my thoughts. "We might be too early."

"Don't you mean late?" I asked, thinking how Seattle's rainy spring often extended into its summer.

"It's not monsoon season," Kinny said by way of explanation.

My blank face must've given me away. Micah, who'd found a walking stick for the journey, lagged behind to join my side. "Spring is cold and dry," she explained. "Monsoon season is August to October, that's the only time it rains besides winter. Usually thunderstorms."

"Cool!"

"Kinny thought maybe it'd already rained up here."

"How do you know so much about Mogollon?"

"Not much else to do," she laughed.

"I mean, same here, but I haven't learned anywhere near as much as you."

"I ask a lot of questions."

We walked in silence for a while, traipsing through the crackly woods. Ravens warned of our approach with deep, guttural croaks. Here and there piles of scat attested to the presence of other, larger, animals.

"Can I ask you one?"

Micah raised her eyebrows.

"Do you ever feel like you don't belong anywhere? Like there's no place for you in this world, that wherever you go you'll always be an outsider?"

"Wow, you don't ask the hard questions, do you," Micah said, smiling. "You're gonna have to give me a minute."

We kept walking, our steps merging into a rhythm, left right left right, walking stick, dodge a tree, back in formation. The minute stretched out to two, then three. I was entirely content to let it stretch to infinity.

"I've got this friend back in college," Micah said, breaking my reverie, "who's been there for over six years. He's changed his major three times already. Three times! His parents have money but that's not the point. The point is, he hasn't found the discipline to stick with anything. And you know what? He's losing confidence in himself because of it. Which makes it even more likely he'll switch programs again, or maybe never get a degree. Whereas if he'd just stuck with the first thing he'd tried…

"I think it's similar when we lose our sense of place, of home. There's this underlying longing we might not even understand, but it gnaws at our inner peace. We don't have a solid foundation to work from. We jump from town to town or job to job, always looking, never finding."

I thought of Lenny Rozier, whose townsfolk and job had jumped away from him instead. I thought of Nick, urging me to commit to something bigger than myself. I thought of Maui, the only home I'd ever known, currently beyond my reach.

"I guess we have to make it for ourselves."

"Exactly!" Micah's smile was pure sunshine. "Nobody can say you don't belong when you feel it in your heart."

I felt it. Oh, I felt it, right there in my heart: the passionate pangs of puppy love. It was a welcome distraction from the existential mess I'd thrust in her direction. And yet she'd taken me seriously the entire time. That had to mean something, didn't it? After all, it wasn't just coincidence we'd landed in Mogollon at the same time. It couldn't be. Coming from Washington State?

We'd have to stay in touch after the summer. Evergreen wasn't so far from Seattle. I began to plot out the future: I'd go back and find a job with another tech firm. We'd get together on weekends and holidays, and eventually fall in love. Once she finished school we'd find a bigger place for the two of us, something near hiking trails – maybe I hadn't liked hiking because I'd never done it with a girl before. We'd visit Mogollon periodically, of course, it being the place that had brought us together, the beginning of our story.

Several hours later we emerged from the forest, having completed an off trail loop and arrived back at the road within sight of our vehicles. Tired and dusty and without having seen a single mushroom, we packed in and drove down the mountain.

They dropped me off in front of my parents' house, Micah dutifully tucking away the slip of paper on which I'd written my phone number. I watched their truck roll down the street, my future love's hair streaming out the passenger window.

I watched my future love lean over and plant a passionate kiss on Marisa's lips.

#

My dreams dashed, my hopes shattered, I dragged my dejected body inside. I was ready for the trip to be over, ready to slink back to Seattle and forget it'd ever happened. They'd been humoring me! Putting up with the teenager's puppy love because it was easier than dealing with his disappointment. Just like Kinny had hired me instead of sending me home, even though I wasn't much use on the job. Well, I was done with all that. I didn't need anyone's pity, or their pithy sentiments. I *would* make it for myself, but not because Micah had said so. Because I couldn't trust anyone else to do it for me.

I opened the door to the sounds of laughter and crying. Ten minutes before the game was set to start, Claus had accidentally sat on the remote control and fried the satellite system.

Chapter Four: Winter 1995

I didn't plan to return to Mogollon that year, but what plans I had made proved unrealistic and unattainable. Between July and November I worked for – and was laid off by – no less than three tech startups. The dot com era was upon us, and though its bubble wouldn't pop for another 5-6 years, for every success story there were a dozen failures you'd never hear about.

I'd managed to pick three in a row.

My meager savings dwindled during these lapses between employment and I was at high risk of losing my apartment and having to move home to live with mother and father again. Except they weren't at home, and I had no desire to live in a ghost town in New Mexico. It was starting to feel like I'd make a mistake in stepping off the well-beaten path of college and student loan debt.

Then my sister called to let me know she was going to Mogollon for Christmas and would love it if I joined.

Upon hearing my dilemma she offered to pay for my ticket, and then let me know there was an extra room available in her house in Portland.

By that point I was ready to leap at any solution, independent or otherwise, so less than two weeks later I left grunge town for stump town and never looked back.

We must've been a sight for those conservative New Mexicans as we rolled into Mogollon, my sister with her blonde crew cut and Queer Nation patch and asymmetrical braid hanging over her left shoulder; and me with jet black hair and cutoffs and combat boots, literally three clichés in a trench coat.

Catron County was entirely unaffected by the burgeoning tech market; its bubble had popped in the 1940s when war scarcity made necessary mining components unavailable. Like Lenny Rozier said, the company town of Mogollon's population had plummeted from several thousand to a few hundred virtually overnight, and thus began the slow decline to its current population of 22.

Still, for whatever reasons, a small core of people hung on. Some had been born there and simply called it home. Others may have had nowhere else to go. And over the years, now and then a visitor would discover exactly what they were looking for, and choose to stay.

The actual definition of a ghost town is hotly debated among enthusiasts, ranging from the strict requirement of being entirely abandoned by humans to the less strident label of a town whose purpose for being no longer exists. Mogollon in 1995 fell into this looser category. The current town was little more than a portion of its original downtown area; cabins and houses and other dwellings had stretched up and down the canyon for miles as well as into side canyons and up hillsides. And if one looked closely enough they'd see evidence of much older habitations than what the miners had left behind.

This was where Apache with names like Victorio and Geronimo roamed. And hundreds of years earlier, a people now called the Mogollon made their home at the Gila

Cliff Dwellings, some forty miles away for the crow and the raven.

This wasn't just a ghost town. It was ghost country.

To my great relief, the house had been updated with a new pump and a gray water system; we were finally able to take showers without the rigmarole of prepping systems and dry soaping. It being winter we weren't even expected to use the outhouse.

The satellite dish, however, had been sold for scrap metal.

On Christmas Eve, Dustin Loftin (Denny's father and the town handyman) borrowed father's 1968 Harvester and hitched a trailer to its rear end. The trailer was stacked with hay bales and, come nightfall, made its way through town pulling a merry crew of carolers. When it reached our house we all rushed to the front door to watch and listen. Kinny and Reese were there along with the novelty brothers and the Lester family, who lived up a side canyon with their three small children, and several adults I hadn't been introduced to.

After the cacophonous orchestra reached its conclusion we were ushered into the back of the hay ride, to my surprise and dismay. I hadn't brought enough warm clothing to account for the frigid New Mexican mountain air. I huddled between my mother and sister as we rumbled down the road.

The caroling ended at the Lester house where we were invited to warm up with hot cocoa by their fireplace. My sister was allowed a quick pour of Schnapps in hers and nobody noticed – or minded, anyway – when she made a face and swapped mugs with me. The adults were getting plastered.

At some point it dawned on me that we were walking home.

#

Dustin Loftin stopped by the day after Christmas to return the Harvester. He was a short, wiry man with long sideburns and a John Deere hat perched atop his head. A perpetual smile adorned his face.

"Strange weather, huh?" he said, rubbing his hands over the wood stove. "We're usually snowed in by now."

"Couldn't say," said father, "I haven't been here long enough to know."

"Y'all got enough firewood?"

"I think so. Over the spring we used what Robert left and it was more than enough. We didn't gather as much this year, but at least I know how the stove works now."

Dustin laughed. "That's important. So how much you got, five, six cords?"

"Oh, no. Two, maybe three? You think we'll need six?"

He shrugged. "It's gonna be a cold winter. Tell you what. I've got some time free tomorrow, why don't the three of us drive up to the Whitewater trailhead? There's a couple dead oaks up there I've been eyeing. We can help each other and both get one."

"Okay," father said, "if you really think it's necessary."

"Better to have it and not need it, you know the saying."

The next morning we followed Dustin up Bursum as if we were leaving town, but when the road crested the mountain we left it to take a small dirt road up the ridge instead. We bumped and bounced along, the Harvester's shock absorbers about as efficient as its heating system. I'd put on two pairs of socks and three cotton undershirts and gloves and a scarf in addition to my normal winter wear, and I was still cold.

"You'll warm up once we start working," father assured me.

"Can't wait," I muttered.

Dustin did all the chainsaw work, cutting down and then cutting up the two trees without seeming to break a sweat, though that may have been the quick work of evaporation. We hauled logs and I discovered that father was only partially right: my core temperature rose to the point that I needed to remove a layer, after which I immediately got cold again. So I replaced the layer and started sweating, which should have cooled me off but just made my clothes stick to my skin. It was a vicious cycle: no matter how I arranged my gear, I couldn't maintain a comfortable temperature. By the time the trucks were loaded I was shivering steadily, and drenched in sweat.

"It's the cotton," father said, "we need to get you in some good old fashioned wool."

"Don't you miss being warm," I muttered, more of an accusation than a question.

"This is very much what I'm used to." Father answered literally, either sidestepping my intent or missing it altogether. "I spent half my life in the cold, remember?"

"Well I didn't."

He didn't respond at once. We bumped down the hill not quite silently, for the truck was having its own conversation.

"It was too much work," he said at last.

"What?"

"Living on Maui. Fitting in there. Finding community. Even after twenty years I never really felt accepted."

"You're an immigrant, you're gonna feel out of place anywhere!"

"It was the same for your mother."

I grunted in frustration and looked out the window. We were almost back in town. "And this is where you went to find acceptance. To be part of a community."

"Hey," father said, his tone serious, "Dustin's a Republican, you know that? He's what many people would call a redneck. We're not going to agree on politics. But he's our neighbor and he came over to check on us. He took time out of his day to make sure we had firewood. You don't get that everywhere."

I tried to remember my neighbors in Seattle. Faces I'd waved at, some I'd avoided. Nobody had ever checked on me during bad weather. But then I'd never done any checking either.

#

I didn't warm up for the rest of the trip, no matter how many layers I put on or how much father stoked the wood stove. There was always some part of my body that was cold.

It snowed the night before we left, a solid four inches blanketing the canyon floor and road and Forerunner. Suddenly the town took on a new aspect: winter sports recreation destination! If I'd had a pair of skis I would've been able to ride them right through town. If I'd had a sled-

But it was time to leave. Albuquerque was a four hour drive in the best of conditions, and getting off the mountain in a timely fashion was suddenly up in the air. Or at the very least dependent on the four inches above the ground.

I shivered as we loaded the Toyota. I shivered as it warmed up in the side yard. And I shivered as we drove down the road, heat blasting on Astrid and father in the front seats. I sat in the back by myself, wondering what to do with my life.

We met the snow plow at the top of the pass. It was an easy ride down the hill from there. The Toyota finally warmed up enough for me to remove my hands from my pockets and loosen my scarf. By the time we reached the high plains all traces of snow had disappeared from the landscape. It must've been even warmer up front because father cracked open the sunroof. Some minutes later Astrid spotted a herd of elk across the road. Father slammed on the brakes so we could stop and marvel at the gorgeous spectacle.

Four inches of fresh snow from atop the Forerunner slid through the crack in its sunroof and completely doused Astrid and father's heads and necks and laps.

I laughed harder than I'd laughed in years.

Chapter Five:
Summer 1997

The old man was turning fifty! Sisters and cousins and children and grandchildren from across the Atlantic were coming to celebrate! My parents' house was packed to capacity, people sleeping in the main hall as well as the two guest bedrooms and the living room. For this week at least, the Fredericksen party had doubled the small town's population.

Danish people are a little different. They will stop whatever they're doing at 2:30 every afternoon and sit down to drink a cup of tea, or coffee, and play a hand of canasta. If they happen to be driving they'll pull over and whip out a camping stove. If they're hiking, same thing. There is not an activity in the world that Danish people won't put on hiatus for afternoon tea.

After a few days of this Astrid, our cousin Annika, and I tired of the routine and asked if we could go on an overnight camping trip down Whitewater Canyon to the Catwalk park, where the adults were planning to visit anyway. We proposed to meet them there in two days' time.

Father drove us up the road to the Deloche trailhead which would lead us out of Silver Creek Canyon and south to Whitewater Canyon – this was a different route than we'd taken for firewood and would give us a longer journey than the actual Whitewater trail.

We had plenty of food and a water purifier and a good tent. It took an hour to crest the ridge between canyons. Then we were skirting yucca and cholla and pincushion cacti, and the occasional blue agave. Nick would've been impressed: I'd dug in and learned their names! The cholla in particular caught my fancy as its dried husk formed a hollow tube with holes along its exterior length, almost like a webbing. I tried to pick one up but it was too young and I got pricked for my effort.

Blue Agave Cactus

Then we dropped below the tree line and into the shade once again, the path finally leveling out to parallel the creek downstream. Whitewater rarely flowed more than a healthy trickle, but when the monsoon hit and it did flood the canyon's sheer walls lived up to their name. We were inside the Gila Wilderness now, the oldest designated National Wilderness in the

United States, and the trees seemed to know it: they erupted overhead like fireworks that never went out. Our feet crunched along the ground, snapping twigs and dried grasses wantonly. There hadn't been a sign of humans all day.

A crashing on the other side of the canyon caught our attention. A black bear dashed out from behind a tree! Before any of us could react it galloped on all fours along the slope and disappeared into the foliage.

We stared at each other, hearts pounding. This was the real deal! If it had been unfriendly... if we'd stumbled upon its cub... if there was another one out there right now...

"It was more scared of us than we are of it," Astrid said, the certainty in her voice reassuring both me and Annika.

We camped at an established site downstream and made sure to hoist our food bag into a tree before sleeping. A large area had been cleared of greenery next to the creek so we felt safe building a fire. Annika told us about college in Denmark and we told her about Portland. She was dating an exchange student from Brazil. Astrid was thinking about moving back to Hawaii. I'd gotten another gig with a tech startup.

As we sat by the fire I whittled on a piece of cholla wood I'd stubbornly coerced from the dead cactus's grasp. It felt good to slide the blade through the wood's outer layer, exposing its inner color. Father had given me his father's pocketknife just before we started hiking. *He would've wanted you to have it.*

We came from a long line of makers and builders: woodcarvers, shipwrights, cabinetmakers, craftsmen. But father had never pushed me to follow in his path. In his own way he'd already broken from the family's traditions, emigrating halfway across the planet. So it had never been an issue that I was more interested in using my hands to work a computer than to hold actual tools. But as I sat there whittling in the near dark by the campfire in Whitewater Canyon, deep in ghost country, something came over me. I could see the wave of future events laid out like a prophecy: if I kept doing computer work it would become my entire life. Maybe this gig would be the one to hit gold or maybe I'd go to college to get trained for a better one, but either way. There was doing business using computers, and there was making computers your business.

And suddenly I wanted nothing to do with them.

We emerged from the wilderness two days later, dripping wet and cleaner than the day we'd left. Whitewater creek formed several small pools at the top of the Catwalk, majestic reflections of boulders and canyon walls shining up at us invitingly. We splashed and swam and washed off the camping dust before making the final trek to the parking lot.

The Danes were having tea, of course.

At the Catwalk parking lot

But back in Mogollon the town was astir! The Lester kids biked up and down Bursum in variously unsafe gear. Dustin Loftin zipped around on an ATV, coordinating logistics and such. Residents I'd never seen before milled about, drawn to the spectacle. Kinny announced a poker tournament on the night of the party.

CALAMITY CANYON

One of the guys I met was John Swede, a hard-boiled Harley rider who'd lost his bike gambling. He had a cabin up the road he'd inherited from his father, his own palace flophouse. He rented a room to Filbert, another old man with a grizzled face and a beer gut who could've been John's twin, but bigger. They did odd jobs sometimes.

There was Powell, the volunteer fire chief, a six foot six beanstalk of a Russian with such bright blue eyes that nobody looked him in the face for fear of falling into their depths and landing in some foreign realm where nobody spoke English and only ate beet soup and potatoes. As a direct consequence Powell, or quite possibly Pavel, stooped when he walked and avoided eye contact when speaking publicly.

There was Reese, of course, buzzing about with the energy of a beehive, as if it was her personal duty to entertain the entire town.

And there came old Bob Maldonado himself, all decked out in cowboy boots and hat, belt buckle gleaming in the summer sun! He was just happy someone had bought his house. It had really been his wife's house, he explained, Hazel was one of the last generation to be born and die in Mogollon. He nodded knowingly at John Swede and Filbert. *This isn't a place for kids to grow up anymore.*

I looked for the Lester kids, but they'd gone home.

On the day of the party a heat wave struck, raising temperatures over 100 degrees Fahrenheit. The main hall in my parents' house, what had once been a dry goods store, then Hazel's art gallery, and more recently the beginnings of a cabinet shop, was cleared in a massive effort and a long table built down its center of various materials including sawhorses and door slabs. This was then covered in paper tablecloths featuring red and white zigzag patterns made by local artists. Chairs were found, and food emerged from what must have been every kitchen in town. The thick stone walls did their best to keep the scorching heat out, but body temperature more than compensated for its insulation value.

At one point Bob Maldonado, in a full body sweat, asked if there might be any ice water. When mother suggested he roll up his sleeves he demurred, shyly admitting that it would expose his long underwear. She took him aside and showed him to the bathroom to remove his under layers before he fainted.

And then, just as we were about to start eating, a troop of belly dancers shimmied their way in the front door!

#

That evening, no longer a minor, I stayed up late drinking whiskey and playing cards with Kinny and Powell or Pavel and John Swede and Filbert and Bob Maldonado at The Tilted Windmill.

Between hands I eyed the tavern's rustic décor, all wrought iron and stained oak and blown glass, turn of the century engineering repurposed as tables and railings and footrests. Elk and deer antlers hung from the walls at random. The building hadn't ever been a windmill, but its rafters and framing came from one that blew over in a storm. Its blades, still intact, decorated the wall behind the bar, a floor to ceiling ornamentation which had required careful disassembly to fit through the door.

"This was a good day," said Reese, counting money behind the bar.

"We need more like it," Kinny replied. "This place was packed every night in the '80s."

Filbert laughed. "You youngsters. I remember when more people lived in Mogollon than Silver City!"

"No you don't," said John Swede.

"There were thirteen bars. I drank from The Bloated Goat!"

"That was before you was born, Paul Bunyan."

Filbert harrumphed. "Well anyway, you could live here. Work your own claim."

John Swede scoffed. "Most people was employed by the company. Maybe they worked a claim on the side, but most of them went broke."

"Well anyway, nowadays there's no work."

"Do you have a website?" I blurted at Kinny.

Everyone laughed at the city slicker. "I don't even have a bank account," Filbert choked out.

"It could draw in a lot more business," I said defensively.

Kinny shrugged. "Publicity doesn't only mean more business. It means more tourists, more traffic, more wear on the road. But it might be necessary."

"More fire danger," Powell or Pavel put in.

"They should stage movies again," Bob Maldonado suggested. "Hazel was an extra in My Name is Nobody, did you know that? She met Henry Fonda!"

"Westerns are dead," Reese announced with certainty, "like mining. They just haven't been told yet."

"Pinchy Pen-DAY-hoe!" John Swede exclaimed, slamming his glass on the table, "are we talking politics or playing cards here?"

After the game I found my way up the street without too much difficulty. The front door was locked so I went around to the side yard and walked up the steps to the back porch. Mother was sitting in a rocking chair, staring out the window at the darkness.

Clara Lynn Fredericksen was not a traditional housewife. The only child of doting Jewish parents, she'd breezed through the social rituals and hierarchies of the mid-60s San Fernando Valley scene, graduating second in her class at Grant High School and segueing that performance into a scholarship to study international business at UC Berkeley.

In her second year she was accepted into a transfer program to the Copenhagen Business School and, against her parents' wishes, left the country for the nine month semester.

She would only spend two in school.

Clara met Thom at a Vietnam protest march. Denmark was one of a few countries without an extradition treaty at the time, so many American men had fled there seeking asylum after being drafted into the military. Thom, who'd grown up on American music and culture, was attracted to the scene without really understanding why they were protesting. She tried to explain the difference between communism and democracy but he was more interested in jazz theory.

Truth be told, Clara hated business school. She hadn't wanted any of the awards or the prestige as a child and didn't want to spend her time in Europe locked in the classroom studying principles of economics written hundreds of years ago by highly privileged noblemen! She'd applied for the transfer program specifically to put an ocean between herself and her parents, and she meant to take full advantage of her newfound freedom.

They spent the next six months hitchhiking through Western Europe, playing music to pay their way, sleeping along the roadside when they had to, never outstaying their visas, eventually making it to the tip of Spain and crossing the Strait of Gibraltar to Tangier.

Sitting on a beach on the way to Casablanca, Clara felt something she'd never felt before but recognized immediately, and knew her life had changed forever. She was going to become a mother. She watched Thom wade in the surf, a beer in his hand as usual, a skinny musician with no plan for the future.

She had plans, though. Children hadn't factored into them yet but that was okay. Maybe it would be better if she returned home with a family. All would be forgiven in the excitement of a grandchild. Her parents would throw an extravagant wedding and they'd walk away with enough gift money to start a household.

Thom took the news stoically. "Bring me to warm water or the mountains," he said, "Denmark has neither."

On the porch, Mother enfolded me in a bear hug that lasted a little too long. "Good party?"

"I won thirty-four dollars," I said. Then I added, "that's more than I made working last week."

"Oh honey," she pouted. "You'll figure it out, you always do. It's in our blood! We don't take the traditional route, you and me."

"Is that what you call hiring belly dancers?"

She laughed, a dry chortle. "Why do you think that was me?"

"Well, anyone else would've worried about offending you."

Even in the dim light I could see a shadow pass across her face. "Wouldn't that be nice."

"What do you mean?"

"I don't come from a big family," was all she said in reply. We sat silently for a few minutes. I was starting to drift off when she sighed. "This year is our twenty-fifth anniversary. It hasn't always been easy."

Too tired to understand what she was trying to say, I said the first thing that came into my mind. "Must be smooth sailing from here!"

Of the many things that happened on that trip, the look on her face is the one I'll never forget.

Chapter Six:
Summer 1999

A lot can happen in two years. You can start a new job, get a promotion, and plot out the rest of your life only to have the company sold out from under you; you can take your severance pay and flee to the sunny shores of Mexico, culminating in a 24 hour bus ride back to the U.S. border where your mother picks you up hungry, broke, and aimless. You can spend two unhappy days in her little house in Silver City trying to understand why she'd rather live on her own before fleeing once again, this time insisting to be left at the edge of town instead of subjecting yourself to a midpoint drop off between your newly divorced parents.

Why spend 27 years delaying the inevitable? Call it when it's done and move on with your life, that's what my cynical mind was saying as I stood next to Highway 180 in the arid desert heat, waiting for a ride.

Eventually an old Toyota Corolla pulled over. The driver barely fit behind the wheel; his long white beard flowed over a bulging belly that peeked out from moth holes in his overstretched t-shirt. Shorts and Birkenstock sandals completed the picture of an off duty Santa Claus. He was only going to Cliff, he informed me, but I was welcome to ride that far. Not many hitchhikers around here.

I told him I was from Maui and the man, whose name was Richie, began to regale me with tales of his childhood on the Big Island, living down in Waipi'o Bay where you could only get by horse drawn carriage or by walking a mile down one of the steepest dirt roads in the world. He was a fisherman then. He used to catch crawdads for fun, wading into streams and reaching under the embankment with one arm to tickle the nests so they'd pinch his fingers. Then he'd whip his arm out and grab as many as he could with his other hand, stuffing crawdads into his mouth when necessary.

One day he'd been submerged up to his neck, crawdads in both hands and more poking out of his mouth, when the daily carriage happened by. A beautiful woman and her young daughter sat erect on the dickey box, the driver on their right. He waved to Richie. *Party on the beach tonight!*

That was when Richie officially met Priscilla and Lisa Marie Presley.

I walked through the blink-and-you-miss-it town of Cliff, figuring I'd have a better chance of a ride on the far side. I was nearly out of drinking water and considering walking back to the gas station when a rancher's truck eased off the road and stopped. I ran to the passenger door but it was locked. The window cracked an inch.

"You going to the hot springs," the man frowned. He wore a button down flannel, blue jeans, and pointed cowboy boots. "They're closed."

I stared at him stupidly. "I don't know any hot springs, I'm visiting my dad in Mogollon."

"What's his name," the man's frown deepened.

"Thom. Thom Fredericksen."

"The cabinetmaker, huh." He thought about it. "Guess I can give you a ride to Glenwood."

His name was Cody McQueen and his family had lived in the valley for five generations. He'd witnessed firsthand the devastating economic effects of environmentalism. "All these damned hippies with their idealism have no idea what it takes to live out here," he informed me. "This is cattle country! Lumber land! These mountains were made for mining – they'll be back, mark my words – and if the damn liberals think they're going to stop them with an owl they've got a fight on their hands."

He dropped me off at Ellie's Country Kitchen, where I ordered a chocolate milkshake and called father to come and pick me up.

As Cody drove away I read the bumper sticker on the back of his truck: Due to the shortage of wood and paper products, wipe your ass with a spotted owl.

#

Father had sunk into a depression when mother left town, binging on cigarettes and alcohol, much like his own father before the aneurysm. John and Filbert were his constant companions now. They played nightly poker games, Father's cabinet shop never quite reaching fruition in the wake of his sorrow. The card games took a constant form: Father would lose to John or Filbert. Not enough to hurt him but easier than a day's work.

I did my best to win it back.

One night Mr. Lester came down from his side canyon to join us. He was the new volunteer Fire Chief, Powell or Pavel having boarded up his cabin and left town on a bicycle earlier that spring. Rumor was he intended to make his way to the tip of Chile or die trying.

Despite the town shrinking to 20 residents, Mr. Lester wanted to expand the volunteer station's rating with the fire department. If they could get everyone in town trained to a certain level, he said, they'd receive more equipment and a larger annual budget. All the guys had to do was attend the training sessions.

"I'm disabled," Filbert reminded Mr. Lester.

"I can't afford to drive to Cliff," John Swede protested.

Father was too far gone to respond, and I, of course, wasn't staying.

"Get your boy to do it," Filbert suggested.

Mr. Lester sighed. "He's off to college in the fall. I'm starting to think old man Maldonado was right."

"Your kids are capable," John Swede said. "I'd take that over a fancy education any day."

"Maybe. Still there's nothing for them here. The girls will grow up and leave too. This town is dying."

"If the price of silver goes up…" John murmured.

"Rock and a hard place," Filbert quipped.

It was strange sitting there with those old-timers, the last of the mining legacy, no less abandoned than the rusting hunks of metal doubling as memorabilia along Bursum road. It was even stranger watching father – watching Thom – turn into one of them. Leftover flotsam from a bygone era. What would the town be without them?

"Good enough place to drink myself to death," John Swede declared, raising his glass. I watched father toast him, a little concerned at the sentiment.

"That's my cue," said Mr. Lester, getting up unsteadily and opening the door. "Sheila," he said in surprise, "I thought you'd left town."

A woman stood outside. Wrinkled, weather beaten features poked out from sandy blonde hair gathered in a mop atop a blue visor. She was short and thin and her hands shook as she stepped into the house. She eyed the unfinished woodshop and the empty whiskey bottles and all the other signs of heartbreak.

"Dusty," she sniffed, "this place needs a woman's touch."

Filbert exchanged a glance with John Swede. "Looks like there's still prospecting to be done in these hills," he chuckled.

Chapter Seven: Summer 2002

The next time I visited New Mexico I didn't go to Mogollon. I'd loaded my Subaru GL with all my belongings and left Portland after finishing a two-year degree, intending to stay with mother for the summer and help her build a greenhouse in her new backyard. She'd wheeled and dealed herself into a large house with acreage on the edge of Silver City, on the road heading to the Cliff Dwellings.

My sister was going back to Maui and the house we'd rented was up for sale. When faced with the thought of moving I couldn't find any reason to stay in Portland. And mom needed help, and I'd been doing handyman work for over five years now. How hard could a greenhouse be?

As hard as the ground you put it on, it turned out. Which was very hard indeed; about as hard as the wind blew, which explained the need for three feet deep holes to set the corner-posts in. And tumbleweeds: it explained tumbleweeds. I'd never realized they could get bigger than a person and completely block a driveway.

The problem was that the ground was rocky, too. Every time I tried to remove a shovel load of dirt, rocks fell from the edge of the hole into the bottom. After several hours all I had was an upside down pyramid of a hole far wider than necessary but still not deep enough, not a cleanly edged hole bored straight into the ground like every hole I'd ever dug in Portland.

I got frustrated. Mom tried to manage me. I got even more frustrated. She suggested she call her handyman for advice. I wanted to ask why she hadn't just had him do the job in the first place. Instead I got into my car and drove off.

Against all odds there was another guy from Maui in Silver City. Brady Webber had moved to New Mexico to help his mother (irony duly noted) open and run a gourmet restaurant. I sat down at a table at Dinah's and ordered a marguerite pizza. After a while Brady came out and joined me. I vented.

"Want to go out to my dad's?" he asked. "I get off in ten."

"What's at your dad's?"

"He lives out by the Cliff Dwellings. We could look for arrowheads."

"I'm in."

We picked up his younger brother and drove the 40 plus miles right up to the National Monument's parking lot before Brady pulled his lifted Toyota off the main road and forded the West Fork of the Gila River. The trail turned into a two track pathway through brush and undergrowth. We forded the river several times, all while Brady and his brother regaled me with childhood stories of trying to cross when the water was high and losing their vehicles, their father swimming out with a rope to save everyone. Then the truck eased between two gigantic rock formations and the land opened up into a beautiful meadow with a log cabin perched beside the river, a veritable pasture of heaven.

"We're closer to your dad's than your mom's right now," Brady said, "but it'd take a lot longer to get there."

"You'd have to walk," his brother explained.

Then they took me on the most rugged hike I'd ever done in my life, climbing up a canyon wall and along the top of a ridge in the hot sun, not an arrowhead or a bottle of water to be seen, then finally scooting back down the canyon on our behinds, the bedrock slick and unforgiving, my head pounding from the sun and dehydration and probably a little bit of guilt if we're being honest.

By the time I got back to mom's it was dark. I begged off dinner and slept straight through until noon the next day. When I finally got it together to put on my work clothes and make an effort to show I was ready to dig again, she let me know that the holes were done. Her handyman had taken care of them.

I went outside to see for myself. Somehow the guy had managed to dig the most beautifully symmetrical holes, three feet deep and just over a foot across, without turning the sites into inverted pyramids or disturbing the rocks that lined the holes like old school wells.

I went back inside and sat down at the kitchen counter. "That guy's really good. Why didn't you just hire him to build the greenhouse?"

"Well of course he could do it," mom responded, "but I figured if I was spending the money anyway I'd rather pay you. And it would be fun to work together!"

For just a moment, I got a glimpse of what it meant to be a wheeler and dealer. You decided how other people could help you and then sold them on doing it.

"I wouldn't have dug those holes," I said, "because I didn't know about the wind conditions because I'm not from here. I would've put the greenhouse on concrete pylons and it would've blown away. When I tried to dig them I failed. If I still go ahead and build the greenhouse, what are the chances I'll do something wrong again?"

"Are you saying you don't want to do it?"

"I'm saying I'm not qualified!"

"Well…" I could see her brain churning. "I could ask Brian, that's my guy's name, if he'd mind you consulting with him."

"Are you kidding?" I exclaimed. "You want me to consult with the guy whose job I'm taking? No way!"

"Maybe you could work together."

I looked away.

"Is this about something bigger? Are you still mad at me for divorcing your father? I have a life too, you know! I have a right to my own pursuit of happiness. I'm not going to mother him for the rest of his life."

"Well maybe you could stop mothering me too!" I yelled.

I glared at her. She stared back.

At last she spoke. "Okay," she said, "I can do that. You're off the hook. I'll hire Brian and you can do your own thing. Stay as long as you'd like."

"Thanks," I said, scowling, not sure how to take the victory. Had I been unreasonable? Why did I feel like the bad guy?

As I sat there stewing, I realized that I wasn't mad at her for divorcing Thom. Or maybe I was, but that wasn't why I was frustrated. Somehow I'd fallen back into the role of the child in the relationship when I'd intended to show up as an adult, a competent person with skills and abilities in my own right. I'd felt patronized by the suggestion that I ask another handyman for help. Even if it was a viable solution she was offering, it wasn't how I'd wanted to show up. And now things had spun way out of proportion.

"Maybe I'll go visit dad," I said, knowing even as the words came out of my mouth that they would hurt her.

"Figured you would, sooner or later." She got up and began tidying the kitchen. "Say hello from me. I really do wish him the best. I hear he's seeing someone. That's good. You can die from loneliness, you know. Robert Maldonado passed away recently."

A few hours later I got into my Subaru and started driving, and both of us knew I wasn't coming back anytime soon. Wherever my home might be, it wasn't at mom's house anymore. What were the chances I would find it at dad's?

When I reached the highway I turned left and headed west.

Part Two

Chapter Eight: Summer 2007

We drove over Safford and Mule Creek into New Mexico, then turned left at the tee towards Glenwood. In the distance gray clouds hovered over the mountains, intermittent arcs of lightning flashing and bolting.

"We might be driving into a storm," I said to my wife.

Tracie glanced in the back, where our two year old daughter Evelyn was snoozing in her car seat. "I like storms."

I pressed on the gas. It had been eight years since I'd been to Mogollon, but I was starting to recognize landmarks and that made me even more eager. Enough of this high desert scrub! Take me to the mountains!

We were five miles from the turnoff to Bursum road when it began to rain. At first they were just little drops so I tapped the rental car's wipers as needed. But soon the little drops turned into big drops and the wipers were running full speed. I was just able to see out the window the rain was coming down so thick. Then, suddenly and mercifully, it stopped.

Only be replaced with hail moments later! This time there was no ramp up, there was just marble-sized hail pelting the landscape and the vehicle at full bore. We slowed to a crawl. Tracie and I exchanged a worried glance. In the rearview Evelyn's eyes were wide open. It was so loud we couldn't have discussed our options if we'd had any.

There was nowhere to hide, not a tree or a building in sight. If the windshield broke we would be completely at the storm's mercy. I could've pulled over to the shoulder but that was it. But pulling over would mean admitting I'd brought my wife and baby daughter into an unsafe situation.

I thought of all the pioneers in their covered wagons, expanding across the country a century or more ago. They'd either thrived or died, there was no in between. Every single one of them had put their families in dangerous situations. Would they have worried about a little hailstorm?

We drove on, though slowly. After several minutes the storm passed. I realized the windshield wipers were working overtime and shut them off. The road was wet. We passed through Glenwood and came to the Bursum road turnoff. I pulled up to the historical marker.

"This is it," I said. "The adventure starts here."

Tracie's eyes widened.

#

Yes, Thom was turning 60 and yes, his Danish family was once again descending on Mogollon for a celebration. Cousins I hadn't seen in a decade milled about town like they'd never left, some with kids of their own in tow. A fierce handstand competition broke out in Thom's sandy side yard. I got admonished for climbing the stone wall and setting a bad example.

Kinny had a new girlfriend, a down to earth pizza chef from Santa Fe. They were trying a new model at the tavern, offering lunch and dinner, hoping it would lead to more business with tourists passing through.

"So," I asked, "what's the town's population now?"

Thom thought about it, counted up and down and back up one hand, then dropped two fingers. "Seventeen."

We were spared the belly dancers this year, but not the Danish tradition of singing song after interminable song once dinner had been served and finished and the tables pushed out of the way. One aunt distributed printed pamphlets of verses (in Danish) while another explained to the American members of the party (in English) what was about to happen.

The Danish language is guttural. They pronounce many of the words and sounds with their throats, adding in higher lilts for the L's and T's and at the end of sentences. The D in my name sounds more like an L, and don't get me started on the Rs! Danes would probably make great didgeridoo players, but the overall tonal effect of their singing is anything but lyrical.

Evelyn loved it though. She rode my youngest aunt's hip the entire evening, singing The Wheels on the Bus, already dancing to her own drum.

Sheila came to the party for an hour before abruptly disappearing for the night. Thom made her excuses; she'd just come down from the fire tower and had a migraine, but later he admitted she just didn't like crowds.

As far as I was concerned she had a free pass: she and Thom were good for each other. The cabinet shop was finally open and he was working again. He'd gone in with Kinny to share the cost of installing UV filtered septic systems in their houses; now we could all poop to our hearts' content, guilt free. They'd adopted a cat, an orange tabby named Hugo. I'd even heard my father playing the guitar again.

Sheila had taken over at fire watch when Reese left the canyon. She was a landscape painter by trade, an artist, and holing herself up on top of a mountain with gorgeous views in all directions was hardly a daunting proposition.

In fact it was far cozier than the room in the little miner's cabin she'd rented from Lenny Rozier beforehand. She still visited him periodically, even after getting the job and moving in with Thom. She might not have liked people in groups but she liked some of them on their own.

As for Tracie, she loved every minute of it. She laughed at the songs and played with the kids as if she regularly got together with dozens of cousins and aunts and uncles.

Then again, considering her small town Mormon upbringing, this was probably a pretty normal gathering.

#

On our last full day in Mogollon I took Tracie and Evelyn up to the Deloche trail for a hike. We'd been on several family walks, but never just us – not that anyone seemed to mind but me. Tracie had taken to my Danish relatives like they were her own, which was legally true but a little disconcerting. It brought out a side of her I'd not seen in our four years together, or more accurately, I learned for the first time that the side of her I was used to – the loving and nurturing wife and mother – extended outward to include every member of my family. Maybe it should've been flattering but I just wanted her for myself again.

We joined a row of out of state vehicles at the trailhead and ambled up the path toward the ridge overlooking Whitewater Canyon, Evelyn cozily strapped to my back in a purple pack. Midday sunbeams twinkled through the forest canopy. Our feet fell softly on the downy ground. At some point over the past decade I'd abandoned my combat boots for hiking shoes and left the trench coat behind. They were part of my life as a techie, which had ended the last time I'd been on this trail, I realized with a start. I'd come full circle.

When we climbed above the canopy I pointed out the different varieties of cacti, sounding out the names for Evelyn. Tracie plopped a sunhat onto her head. We shared a swig of water. She'd packed energy bars for us and snacks for Evelyn but we wouldn't be out long enough for a full lunch.

A group of hikers passed us on their way down, day trippers like ourselves. Tracie smiled and greeted each person in passing.

"They have the minivan," she said a few minutes later.

I laughed. "The accent!"

"Texans for sure."

It became a game: guess the hikers' state from their accent. Tracie won two out of three (to the best of our knowledge as we didn't actually ask) before we reached the top of the ridge and the trail started down to Whitewater.

"This is as far as we go." I turned in a circle to take in the view. The ground fell away to both sides of us, the ridge protruding from the mountain like a skeletal finger. Ravens and turkey buzzards flew in the distance. Far below, another group of hikers made their way up the trail.

"Look," I said, pointing at the lay of the land below us, "that's where we came from. That's where the car is parked. And that's where the road goes after the trailhead. I've been up there with Kinny and some friends. How about instead of taking the trail back, we walk up the ridge for a minute and then cut down *here*," I stabbed a finger at a gulley in the hillside, "and follow it down to the road. We can't miss it. That way we're not backtracking, and there won't be other hikers."

Tracie pursed her lips, considering. "I'm not sure it's a good idea. Nobody will know where we are if something goes wrong."

"Nothing's gonna go wrong, we're just taking a shortcut back to the car. Which is right there, and we told everyone where we were going so they'd know where to look if something did go wrong. The general area anyway. But nothing's gonna go wrong!"

Tracie grudgingly agreed, or didn't argue in any case, so I led us off the trail and up the spine of the ridge, weaving between cacti and scrub brush and tufts of grasses. Deer and elk poop littered the ground.

"Look, an animal trail," I said triumphantly, "going our direction no less!"

We followed the track down the north face of the canyon. It was easy going, like the animals knew the way better than the Forest Service.

"What do you have against people?" Tracie said suddenly, her tone indicating she'd been stewing over the question for some time. "It's like you want to live on an island with no one but us."

"Would that be so bad?" I joked, stalling. I wasn't sure what to say. I'd thought that's what marriage was, a metaphorical island, a special bond between two people that nobody came between except their own children. So I wanted a little time with my family. Why was that a bad thing?

"It's not funny," Tracie insisted. "We only get so many chances to see your relatives, we should be spending every moment with them. Not out here chasing who knows what!"

I thought of, and rejected, several responses to the implied question. "I don't have anything against people," I said, picking my words carefully, "but there's things we'll miss if we stick with the group the whole time. The quiet, for one. There's always someone talking! This hike for another. It would've taken two days to plan and ended up being some tame picnic with tea and canasta."

"Well, this would never fly with my family. Going off and doing our own thing."

I didn't answer. She'd left the church and its community but anytime she disapproved of something I'd done she would hold up her family as a shining example of why I was wrong.

As if to mimic the looming storm of our conversation, dark clouds appeared high up on the mountain. At nearly the same moment our trail dipped below the tree line and the temperature dropped by several degrees. I looked for the gulley. It seemed like we were already in it, but I'd been distracted by the conversation and hadn't kept a close track.

"We should go down here," I said, cutting off the game trail.

"Are you sure?"

I stopped to look back at Tracie, catching a glimpse of Evelyn's snoozing face in my peripherals. "You got a better idea?"

She shrugged. "I *did*."

I shrugged back. "Sorry I got you into this terrible mess."

"Fred, can we just get to the car please? I'm in no mood to argue right now."

"Fine."

We tramped down the bottom of the gulley in silence. It was a natural declivity in the greater plane of the slope, a flood channel for monsoon season, though the grass and shrubbery in its bed suggested it had been years since it saw usage. In places it steepened and we had to slide down by squatting and leaning against the mountain carefully, hands braced for support. Evelyn woke up during one such event and giggled at our crab walk.

Then the gulley opened up to merge with a trickling creek.

"This is it!" I exclaimed, panning about, searching the area, "the road should be around here somewhere!"

Tracie declared a pause. She took Evelyn out of the backpack and passed out snacks and energy bars. We drank the last of our water.

"I could look for the road," I suggested, "I'm faster without a backpack."

"Fred Fredericksen, you are *not* leaving us alone in the woods!" Tracie exclaimed.

I held up my hands in surrender. We got Evelyn into her pack and onto my shoulders and started making our way down the creek bed. It was slow going. We had to step from rock to rock within the confines of the creek or hug one of its sloping sides, loose scree slipping under our soles as we scrambled past.

"The wind's picking up," said Tracie.

I'd noticed it the same moment. At first it'd been a warm breeze, then a gust, but now the wind was whipping all about us, bending trees and flinging twigs downwards and back into the air like a maniacal leaf blower. Clouds rolled down the mountain.

The sky lit up with a simultaneous crack of thunder, an explosion like jet planes colliding. I nearly fell to my knees in shock. Reverberations echoed through the canyon, causing rocks and dirt to settle downwards, stop motion avalanches across eons.

Raindrops started falling. I couldn't tell if my eyes were playing tricks or if the water was actually rising.

"We probably shouldn't be in the creek," I said, trying to keep the tremor out of my voice.

"There's nowhere to go!" Tracie yelled.

She was right. To one side the canyon was a sheer slope, the other an interminable scree field. We'd be as likely to start a landslide as climb to safety there. Still, if worst came to worst…

"Let's keep moving," I said, the intertwining goals of appeasing my wife and getting our daughter out of the creek before the water rose acting as both carrot and stick.

"It better not hail," she muttered darkly.

Evelyn began to sob.

"It's okay," I soothed, "daddy's here, we're gonna be fine."

But my actions were hardly soothing. I hurried down the creek, taking chances, stepping on unstable stones and getting my feet wet. So what? The rest of my body was already soaked.

"We'll be fine," I said, still talking to Evelyn, "we'll get through this and daddy will never put you in an unsafe situation again, I promise."

Another flash in the sky. Another crack of thunder.

Evelyn shrieked.

A brief silence ensued. Then a voice filled it. "Hey, you down there! Y'all okay?"

I craned my neck to find the source of the sound. A minivan idled partway up the scree slope, barely twenty feet from us. A pale face peered out the window.

"That the road?" I yelled.

The tourist nodded. "Parking lot's up yonder a ways," he said, pointing the way he'd just come. "Didn't I see y'all on the trail? How'd you get down here?"

"No GPS," Tracie called out, a touch of irony in her voice. She wiped rain off Evelyn's forehead. "Come on, let's go home."

I followed her up the slope, noting the minivan's license plate was from Missouri. I didn't mention it to Tracie.

Chapter Nine: Summer 2012

Sometimes the thing that turns you into a better version of yourself is also the thing nobody can forget about who you used to be. After getting Tracie and Evelyn lost in the woods I'd kept my promise and never put either of them in danger again. I did everything I could to set my own needs aside and follow their lead. I dug into the role of fatherhood in ways I'd never known were possible. We visited her Mormon family without a single day to ourselves and I didn't even grumble.

None of it was enough. I would always be the person who'd gotten Tracie and her 2 year old daughter lost in the woods.

I'd had hours to brood over this paradox as I flew into Phoenix once again, though not for any celebratory reason this time. I was being divorced and my handyman business was in danger of going under, and I was there to help Thom do a cabinet job to make sure I didn't lose my house as well.

I stared out the window as he caught me up on all the local gossip. The novelty shop was closed. Mr. Lester had resigned as volunteer fire chief. Dustin Loftin was in charge now, and he relished the sense of purpose. He'd drive around on his ATV with a weed eater, keeping the road clear of brush and debris, an official Fire Chief hat perched jauntily atop his head.

Only once in all the time Thom lived there had an actual fire started in town. It was the dead of winter and a newcomer hadn't gathered enough wood. He took to burning chairs and furniture to stay warm, and at some point stuck a table leg out too far before falling asleep. The entire building burned, though the man and his four dogs got out okay. They were no longer in town.

"John Swede passed away," Thom said, clucking sadly. "He just didn't want to have anything to do with anyone anymore. Filbert was there of course, he called the ambulance – it took two hours to arrive – but John was unconscious by the time they got him to the hospital. He must've woken up at some point because he heard the nurses saying, *this guy isn't going to last long.* So he sat up, ripped off his oxygen mask, and shouted F- you! and stormed out. He *didn't* last long after that, but he wasn't about to die in the hospital."

"I'd guess that's why people come to a place like this," I said, thinking of Tracie's words when I'd told her I was going to Mogollon. *You'll fit right in.* "Either running from something or to it."

"Maybe," Thom said hesitantly.

"What's the population?"

He didn't have to think. "We're down to twelve full time residents. A doctor bought up John's house along with several other properties. He's building a dream home for his wife, that's whose cabinets we're making."

"He must be employing the whole town."

"And then some. He brought in his own painters from Texas over the winter, but they didn't last long. Once we build these cabinets he's going to have them shipped to Houston to be painted."

"You're kidding," I said, missing the irony of being imported labor myself.

Thom shrugged. "Money does strange things to people."

#

Hugo was no longer with them. "A coyote or a raccoon probably," said Sheila matter-of-factly, "cats don't live too long out here." Her speech was clipped and precise, like she'd calculated the fewest syllables necessary to make her point. She'd retired last fire season and now spent her time painting and hiking. Lenny Rozier had passed away and left his cabin in her name, so grateful was he for her company. His children, however, weren't so thrilled to learn about his will and took her to court, whereupon the judge admonished them for not spending enough time with their dad.

To both of our relief Thom and I worked well together. Between cutting and sanding and planing we bonded over the mutual loss of our kids' moms. It made us equal somehow, not father and son but just two guys who'd loved and lost. And seeing him thriving let me know things would improve for me too, once I got through the painful part.

One day we decided to have lunch at the Purple Onion, a new cafe the doctor had opened across the street. The building was a purple and green striped abomination, but the food was excellent. An adjacent building had been painted bright yellow and given a red tin roof. The overall effect was jarring in the vicinity of the rusting old miners' homes and the doctor's new bungalow mansion, like they'd been somehow lifted out of the magical land of Oz and slightly overshot Kansas.

The yellow and red building had been dedicated to cemetery archives. Admission was free.

"Do people actually go in there?"

"Oh yeah," said Thom. "You wouldn't believe how into it some people get about their genealogy! Once I had a guy knock on the door and ask if my house used to be a bar, he was looking for his great-grandfather's grave and had heard he used to own a bar in these parts, or be a bartender anyway. I sent him up to the graveyard and sure enough, he came back a couple of hours later ecstatic! He'd actually found it. Then he wanted to know where the bar was and I said, *which one? There were thirteen in the heyday. But you should check out The Tilted Windmill, the owner actually got it declared an historic site. There's a plaque on the front.* So the guy goes down the street and comes back a few minutes later even more ecstatic! His great-grandfather's name was actually stamped on the plaque."

"It's really weird there's two restaurants here with only twelve people," I pointed out.

"That's the doctor. I think he's trying to convince his wife to move here full time."

"Ah."

"It's a nice place," Thom said, then paused to qualify the statement.

"But not if you like shopping," I finished.

"No," he laughed, "not if you like shopping."

"Five hours to Phoenix or Santa Fe."

"Oh, I'm sure they fly in. There's an airstrip on the Mesa."

"Ah."

"No, it's that there's no emergency services. No hospital within an hour. If something happens out here that's pretty much it."

"But he's a doctor!"

"A brain surgeon. Very specialized."

"You're telling me a brain surgeon can't do CPR? Deal with a snake bite? Set a bone?"

"I don't know," Thom said, getting a look that told me he did know, "what if something happened to him?"

#

I flew back to Portland near the end of April. The cabinets were built and it was time to return to my real job, both as a father and a small business owner. A chapter of my life had ended, and once again the town of Mogollon had served as a safe haven, a port between storms. Hopefully there wouldn't be any more for a while.

Then, out of the blue one fine day in the latter half of June, Thom called to tell me not to worry, he and Sheila were okay.

It was not reassuring.

Lightning strikes in the mountains had sparked two separate wildfires, which had grown so large they'd merged into one, the Whitewater-Baldy Complex. It was growing by 20,000 acres a day, had already burned dozens of homes, closed the Cliff Dwellings National Monument, and was now bearing down on Mogollon. Over 900 firefighters were assigned to the fire, a large percentage tasked with protecting the town. They'd pitched camp on the mesa and were pursuing multiple lines of mitigation. They cut breaks in the forest line. They tried back burns but the wind was too shifty. They stockpiled water throughout the town in tanks, tubs, and even kiddie pools when they found them. They brought in helicopters when they could, but the fire was too massive. It raged down the mountain, through Whitewater Canyon where I'd camped with my sister and Annika, and up the slope to the very edge of Silver Creek Canyon itself.

By this point Thom and Sheila and the rest of the remaining townsfolk had evacuated to the mesa. Dustin Loftin brought his trailer and helped load Thom's power tools; they were sitting in the sun at a friend's house, the trailer commandeered for further loads.

That night a freak wind blew in from the west, from down the mountain. It hit the mesa first, and hard. It lifted every single firefighter's tent out of the ground and flung them into Whitewater canyon. If they hadn't been out fighting the fire they probably would've been flung into the canyon too, so fierce was the wind. Thom's tools lay in disarray but miraculously nobody was hurt.

The next day the fire crew came down from the mountain, victorious: the break at the top of the ridge had worked! Flames had rushed up the canyon wall and ran out of fuel just as a counter wind pushed the center of the fire back onto itself. It was far from over but barring further calamity the town was safe.

As for their encampment, well. They had to make do with Glenwood's armory for the rest of the job.

Chapter Ten:
Summer 2014

The words *barring further calamity* should never be uttered after a wildfire, because it's not really a further calamity when the consequences of that wildfire can be clearly traced – even predicted – to cause erosion and flooding. Though, to be fair, the summer of 2013 brought a hundred-year monsoon season; *it* couldn't have known that nearly 300,000 acres of the Gila National Forest was completely denuded of foliage and thick with ash, soot, and charred debris, just waiting for a vehicle to propel them down the mountain in a nightmare torrent.

Mr. Lester saw it first up in his side canyon. He called Dustin Loftin. "It's coming," he said. "Tell everyone to get to high ground. There's no way out. "

Dustin Loftin lived halfway up the canyon wall. He went outside and saw the creek was about to overflow. He called Thom. "You'd better move your truck or you're going to lose it," he said.

CALAMITY CANYON

Thom went out and opened the gate to his side yard. As he pulled the Harvester into the street water lapped at its tires. He pressed on the gas and sputtered around the corner of the Old Kelly Store. It was out of the water's direct path now. But that water had already claimed the road and was still rising; he had to jump from the store's porch onto his own to get home.

For the first time since he'd moved in Mogollon, Thom fetched the special sheet of plywood that fit in the grooves set in his cement railing and across the front steps. Now the house could repel an extra two feet of flooding.

Not one minute later a gigantic wave of blackened, deadly water tore through the town, slamming into the side of the Old Kelly Store after all, ripping out bridge after bridge as boulders and branches and tree trunks pushed their way downhill. Houses with foundations were swamped while old miners' cabins collapsed completely. For a time The Tilted Windmill lived up to its descriptor, then it succumbed to the undercutting torrent and collapsed. The road disappeared, not covered in water but its entire structure eroded, hah, sent downstream like so many pebbles and twigs.

The flood

One man tried to drive out. His jeep was found downstream a ways, his body several miles further.

When the water finally receded to the point of being able to leave the house safely, Thom and Sheila discovered they weren't able to; their front steps ended abruptly at a twenty foot drop into the bottom of a new creek bed that stretched all the way across to the front steps of Dr. Kerr's demesne. They had to climb higher up the canyon and hike along its side to get to Dustin Loftin's house and the fire station. From there they surveyed the damage.

The road no longer existed. The bottom of Silver Creek Canyon *was* the creek bed and not a bridge spanned its width. Leaving town was impossible. Not for the first time in its history, the residents of Mogollon were stranded.

Incidentally, a similar event happened in Silver City in 1895: a flood tore through the creek running down Main Street, wiping out all the businesses on one side and leaving behind The Big Ditch, a euphemism at the time for the Panama Canal. The businesses on the other side of Main Street, the ones whose front doors gaped over nothingness like Thom's, boarded them up and began accepting business in the rear. Today the city's main drag is Bullard street, one block over from The Big Ditch.

Mogollon had no such luxury. Most houses' backdoors were holes dynamited into the mountain for cold storage – a small but useful consolation over the next few weeks.

#

By the time Evelyn and I came to visit in the summer of 2014 the road had been repaired enough to drive in and out with four wheel drive. This was entirely the doing of Dustin Loftin and Dr. Kerr, working hand in foot: the one handling the heavy machinery and the other footing the bill.

Maybe what every small town in America needed was a billionaire benefactor, someone more interested in leaving a legacy than extracting value; someone who wanted to be remembered for having done good by the people who lived there. In any case, it was a bumpy ride. Silver Creek was no longer bridged but forded in the center of town. The Harvester was still coughing along, though its internal mechanisms were never quite the same after the trauma of the flood. When the water finally receded it had been found wedged between a black walnut tree trunk and an alder, but intact.

Thom made sure to cut them up for firewood.

How do you entertain a nine year old in a ghost town that's just experienced two massive natural disasters (or one disaster with a year-long intermission)? The Catwalk was closed, maybe permanently, its ancient rigging shipwrecked downstream somewhere in the high desert. The much hyped Purple Onion was inaccessible. Grandpa Thom was starting to lose his hearing and Sheila had never had kids; she didn't know how to relate to them.

The answer turned out to be a little bit prickly: Evelyn was fascinated by cacti. She wanted to find as many as she could, so every time we went for a walk we'd look for new specimens. She was very impressed I knew so many by name.

On the day we helped gather firewood we found the mother lode: a group of flowering blue agave. They towered above us, long stalks with hands of flowers opening up like bananas, hues of reds and yellows contrasting with the greens and blues of the stalk itself.

"What's gonna happen to the town," I asked Thom one evening, "is this the end of Mogollon? Are you and Sheila moving?"

"Oh, no." A funny look crossed his face. "To hear the people around here tell it, the disasters aren't over yet. First there was a fire, then a flood, and next it's the feds. That'll be the end of Mogollon."

"I don't understand."

"A ton of money has been budgeted to rebuilding the town's infrastructure," he explained. "Companies are bidding on the contracts now."

"But won't that save Mogollon?"

"For who? The twelve of us that live here? Nine hundred firefighters and millions of dollars in road contracts? Come on, Frederic. The government doesn't care about us that much."

I chewed on it for a while. "They want something back from their investment."

"Everybody wants something back from their investment."

"You think they'll reopen the mines?"

He shrugged. "It's been talked about. But you can't mine without roads."

"And a town needs roads."

"Yeah."

"Is it even a ghost town then? If it still exists for the same purpose?"

#

A stray kitten was living underneath the Old Kelly Store, a long-haired calico with a funny habit of tilting its head, like it was trying to make sense of things. It would creep out and peer at us but never make noise or let anyone close. Evelyn made a firm decision to befriend it. She borrowed some canned tuna and began baiting the kitten, sitting outside on the porch for hours, talking softly and letting it approach without moving a muscle. Her patience was astounding.

After two days of near misses, of frustrating distractions and more bits of tuna sacrificed, she finally managed to pet the kitten. It trusted her after that, so long as she kept the tuna coming.

One morning I sat on the far side of the porch and watched the kitten, which she'd named Spork, eat its breakfast and get its unruly hair brushed. It had been twenty years since I'd stood in that same spot and watched Denny skin a rattlesnake. Last I'd heard he was a Navy Engineer, sailing around the world working on large equipment.

The sound of hooves clopping against hard earth distracted me from my reverie. I craned my neck just as Evelyn gasped.

"Dad, look!"

A man on a horse – and leading two more – had forded the creek and was approaching our front porch. He was tall and thin and wore a Mexican poncho, a five gallon hat, buckskin chaps and spurs. He stooped in his saddle and spoke toward the ground, nearly hiding his bright blue eyes.

"Hola amigos, my name's Paolo. You know what happened here?"

"Powell!" I gasped. "Or Pavel. Paolo. Whatever. You remember me? We played poker together."

"Ah, the city slicker. I heard you got lost in the woods."

Evelyn giggled.

"How did you hear that?" I demanded. "I thought you were biking to Chile."

"These are better transportation," Paolo said, patting his mare gently. "We go slowly and don't miss as much."

Thom joined us on the porch. "Heard you were back," he said. "Sorry about your cabin."

Paolo shrugged. "You know where this doctor lives?"

Thom pointed out Dr. Kerr's bungalow. "You got a lame horse or something?"

"Well," said Paolo, patting the horse beside him, "these two pass the eyeball test. That one," he jerked a thumb at his trailing companion, "assed the piebald test."

He clicked his tongue and his horses – and mule – began prancing up the road.

"Can't believe he heard I got lost," I muttered incredulously.

"You got *us* lost!" Evelyn corrected.

I conceded the point. "How'd you know he was back?" I asked Thom.

"Oh, it's a small town. Word travels fast."

"But he just got here!"

Thom winked at Evelyn, who giggled at my frustration. "Mr. Lester saw them a few days ago outside of Silver City. I've been wondering when they'd make it to town."

"What will he do?" I wondered. "His cabin's ruined. There's nowhere to stay in town."

"Oh, I'm pretty sure they're self-sufficient. Did you see those saddlebags? I'll bet they've got everything they need with them. They could wander up the road and disappear into the wilderness for months and be totally fine."

"Cool!" said Evelyn, her eyes gleaming.

"Hey, we might've been fine for months, you don't know," I said half-jokingly.

Evelyn giggled again.

A few minutes later Paolo and his team came back down the street. "Adios muchachos," Paolo said, tipping his hat politely, "we're off to Alaska."

"Just like that?" said Thom. "What about your cabin?"

"Es el doctor's now! Buen viaje!"

Paolo tipped his hat again. He clicked his tongue and the team trotted off. We watched them ford the creek and disappear down the street, the clatter of their hooves lingering like a ghostly presence. Then the dust settled and even that was gone.

Chapter Eleven:
Summer 2018

A few days after the end of her seventh grade year Evelyn and I traveled to Mogollon to lend a hand gathering firewood again. Over the winter Thom had slipped on some icy steps in his yard and broken his hip. He didn't know it at first, and limped around for a couple of days until Sheila insisted she drive him to the doctor's office in Reserve. They sent him to the hospital in Socorro, who sent him to a specialist in Albuquerque who ended up entirely replacing the right side of his hip.

Dr. Kerr hadn't managed to convince his wife to spend winters in Mogollon, so the question of whether or not he could set a bone remained open.

As for the town itself, it had indeed changed with the rebuilding of the road. The creek was still close to twenty feet deep, but contained, its sides engineered of interlocking concrete blocks reinforced with steel stakes driven into bedrock. A two-lane bridge spanned its width in the center of town, and, as before, smaller bridges provided access to houses and businesses located across the creek from the road.

The remains of The Tilted Windmill had been bulldozed and cleared. Kinny was in Santa Fe with his girlfriend.

The Purple Onion was open and thriving. Tourists lounged at its picnic tables or wandered through the archive building.

Thom had suspended an ancient handsaw above the entrance to his house with 'Mogollon Woodworks' stenciled on its face. He'd taken to constructing wooden platters and puzzles and scrap mobiles to sell. It was easier on his hip than cabinetry, or, as he liked to joke, he could sit down on the job.

There were even two new residents in town! A retired couple from San Diego had been fortunate enough to snatch up a property before Dr. Kerr heard of its availability. It was up on the hill by Dustin Loftin's house, an old miner's bungalow. But as it turned out the building wasn't entirely on their lot, in fact fully half of it had been constructed on a neighbor's property. Either surveyors hadn't been very precise back then or there was some other story; in any case the new owners, Jayne and Jackson Curry, had to negotiate with that neighbor to buy half of their house a second time! And then pay to have it moved and set on a new foundation.

Platters by Mogollon Woodworks

"Your mom wanted to buy that house," Thom told me, a look of relief on his face; "it gets good sun and is out of the flood plain."

Spork, unfortunately, was no longer around. He'd never taken to anybody but Evelyn and when road construction started the noise drove him away.

The Catwalk park had been rebuilt, its rigging now steel walkways you could look through to the creek below – not as historic but undoubtedly safer.

And up above town, where Fanny Hill road forked to the cemetery and the old mine, a Canadian company was doing exploratory drilling to determine whether it would be worth reopening operations.

"It's nice of you to come and help," Thom said.

We'd loaded his chainsaw into the back of his Toyota, which I'd be driving – the Harvester had too many quirks and this would just be easier, he'd said. He and Sheila had a permit to cut up to 10 cords of downed firewood each per year, though they rarely needed so much; they usually took one truck at a time so they could be together, but with our help we could gather twice as much per trip. We would be heading up the mountain toward Bear Wallow, where we'd gone mushroom hunting so many years ago.

"Well," I said, "half the times I've come here for help. It'll be nice to return the favor."

"The road's not in great shape."

I shrugged. Bumpy was bumpy, right?

The portion of Bursum road we were taking had been built around 1894 by prisoners working for a dollar a day at the direction of then-Sheriff Olaf Bursum, as part of an economic development plan to build a ski resort on Whitewater Baldy. It was entirely a coincidence that the road also represented the most direct route between Mogollon and the town of Reserve, where the Sheriff was stationed – and entirely a fluke that the ski resort never came into being.

CALAMITY CANYON

The New Catwalk

About a mile out we passed the last miner's cabin within town limits, an aging green building surrounded by overgrown shrubbery and derelict vehicles. We passed the parking lot for the Deloche trailhead, now blocked and inaccessible due to fire and flood damage. Then the road left the creek bed and began to wind upwards.

There are two ways to drive up a mountain: if it has a slight slope and you have a big engine you can take the direct approach, or if it has a broad face you can switch back and forth in gentle curves. The more sheer the slope, the tighter the curves and the thinner the road.

I hadn't remembered the road being so narrow and the slope so steep, but then I'd been infatuated with two older girls at the time. Now, as I glanced at my daughter in the passenger seat, all I saw was the paleness in her face as she eyed the stark chasm mere inches from her window.

Ahead of us, Thom and Sheila bumped along without hesitation.

We came across a place where the road had partially washed out; we had to hug the mountainside, almost drive up the embankment, to pass it safely. I began to worry about coming down with a load of oak in the back.

"I don't like this very much," Evelyn said.

"Me neither," I agreed. I flashed my lights and honked the horn. The other truck kept going.

Having little option, we followed.

What seemed like an eternity later we came to a place where the slope eased off and there was enough space to pull over. Far ahead, almost out of sight in the summer dust, I could just see the Harvester. I flashed my lights again. But when the dust cleared, it was gone.

By the time Thom's old truck finally appeared fifteen minutes later, I was livid. I'd put my daughter in an unsafe situation again. "You have to tell people what they're getting into!" I yelled. "You expect me to drive a truck I'm not used to down a mountain road that's half washed out with a full load of firewood?"

"It is safer with the weight," Sheila pointed out.

I waved her off. "Then you left us here! I was signaling you! What were you doing just leaving us here?"

"I thought you wanted us to go ahead because of the dust," Thom explained.

I was too ticked off to hear it. I told them to get their own firewood and drove back down the mountain. We got all the way to Mogollon before I realized we still had the chainsaw.

Chapter Twelve:
Fall 2023

For his 75th birthday Thom and Sheila traveled to Denmark for a change, arriving just in time for a massive heat wave. The high tech light rail they were riding across the country stalled due to overheated micro circuitry, and because the power was down there wasn't any air conditioning. They were stuck for over six hours in excruciating heat in a stuffy rail car, a horrible odor assaulting their senses even further. This turned out to be Thom's sandals, but by the time they'd finally reached his cousin's flat and noticed the odor had followed them, both he and Sheila had fallen ill from heat exhaustion.

The rest of the trip was a blur. On the day of their flight Sheila was throwing up and overtly white in the face, but insisted they not stay longer. She survived all the way to Albuquerque, then collapsed and was hospitalized for a week.

I offered to come out and help around the house but Thom said they'd be okay. I understood. You didn't just show up in Mogollon and help out. You also needed help, unless you had a billion dollars or were entirely self-sufficient. I was neither, and the energy it would've taken him just to get me oriented enough to provide assistance was better spent resting and recovering.

Also, I didn't have a great track record of following through.

So another year went by and it could've been several more before I visited except Astrid decided to make the trip herself, and as it had been many years since we'd last been together I decided to take advantage of the opportunity and visit for a quick week.

A few days later Thom called and asked if I wanted to stay for a month instead. He'd been offered a big cabinet job and was going to need help. We talked it over and got excited about working together again. I was on the verge of changing my ticket when he messaged me to wait. The owners were having trouble choosing a design and the job would be on hold for a while, possibly indefinitely.

A week it was, then. I flew into Phoenix and cruised across the desert in a red Mustang. It didn't overheat on the way up Bursum. It didn't have a name either, I joked to my sister upon arrival.

"Did it rain?" she shot back.

When the American Fredericksens got together we played cribbage instead of canasta. Thom took out the antique wooden board he'd found in the house, its oak and walnut inlay as tight as the day it was made by (or for) one Dan A. Bechtol, whoever he may have been.

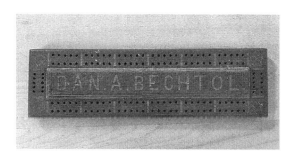

Cribbage Board

"You ever think of making cribbage boards?" I asked.

Thom hemmed and hawed. "Not sure it's that popular a game."

"What if you made a Mogollon deck of cards?" my sister asked.

I laughed. "Dr. Kerr for king!"

"The doctor passed," Sheila informed us. "Heart disease."

"Oh snap!"

"Dustin Loftin passed too, all of a sudden. A stroke."

"That's terrible!" My sister said.

"What does it mean for the town?" I asked, thinking of the lawsuits that followed in the wake of the Gates divorce. "Who's gonna run the cafe?"

"He willed it to Mary Loftin," Thom said. "Dustin's widow."

"That was kind."

"I really think he wanted to help the town. When he put in a well he offered to connect it to everyone's houses."

"Must've been a big well."

"Tell me about it! I think he went 160 feet deep."

"How deep is yours?"

"Mine is a dug well. Hand dug, you know? Then lined with rocks. The idea is groundwater seeps between the rocks and fills up the hole. It's maybe twenty feet deep. Wells nowadays are drilled down to the water table."

"But yours still works."

"Seasonally. It used to be good all year but went dry around the time the doctor put his in."

"Wait, you're telling me the doctor's well dried up yours?"

"It was working one day and went dry the next. It's never been the same."

"Holy cow. So did you connect to his?"

"Yeah, and you know what? I'm the only person who did."

"Nobody trusted him?"

"Nobody wanted to rely on him. Nothing comes without strings."

"And now he's dead."

"Yeah," Thom said, the look on his face somewhere between bemused and concerned.

"But his wife is okay with the arrangement."

"Oh, I think she'll honor his wishes. You know, they have to show they're using the water and nobody lives there. So in a way I'm helping them out."

"What?"

At that point Thom launched into a long winded explanation of water rights and how they're transferable between properties in rural New Mexico. Apparently Dr. Kerr had bought up five sets of water rights, each allowing him to pump a million gallons of water out of the ground per year for agricultural or commercial use. The rights had to be attached to a piece of real property but the water did not have to be used on that parcel. However, if the owner did not use a certain percentage of the million gallons each month (per water right), they would be at risk of losing the rights altogether – and meters had been installed which required monthly reporting.

These rights, incidentally, were entirely separate from domestic use. You were allowed to use water from your own property inside of your house without any sort of additional rights amended to the title. However, this did not apply to any sort of gardening or agricultural usage. Without a separate water right you were literally breaking the law if you grew tomatoes outside of your house. And Thom swore this was true because Kinny had been reported by his neighbor during their feud for exactly that infraction.

"Why?" Astrid asked. "Why did he buy up all these rights?"

"Oh, he wanted to start a bottled water company."

#

We drove up to the cemetery to cut down some trees for firewood. Thom and Sheila always kept an eye out for deadwood on their walks and hikes, and this road was far less intense than upper Bursum. Ravens swooped and croaked at us as we made our presence known. Thom pointed out some trees that had been felled across the road and subsequently dragged out of the way. He thought it had been the Forest Service doing the cutting.

The miners were still performing their exploratory drilling in and around the area, had in fact received permits from the government to expand beyond the footprint of the original mining operations from a hundred years before, right up to the edge of the Gila Wilderness. Thom and Mr. Lester and a few folk from Glenwood, with the help of a group of Chiricahua Apache, were protesting the operation for the sake of ecological sustainability. Aside from the material debris left behind and the gigantic holes in the ground, mining and refining ore was a dirty process which often left watersheds damaged for millennia.

At times they found allies within certain arms of the government. Usually, however, county and state and even federal officials were indifferent. One time Mr. Lester got a meeting with one of Catron County's commissioners, who told him not to worry, it probably wouldn't progress pass the exploratory phase. "One in a thousand of these things ever turn into real operations," he said, "this is just about the contracts."

It took a minute to understand. Let's say somebody buys a piece of property that has mineral rights attached to it. This means they have a legal claim to what's below the ground. They can lease those mineral rights out to a company that has the ability to determine if there's enough gold or silver or other valuable ore in the ground to make it worth mining; this is called exploratory drilling. Such a company, before doing any work, will sell this package of opportunity, this prospect, to someone with enough money to back a mining operation in the event they do strike gold.

If only one in a thousand of these exploratory contracts turned into a real operation, neither the land owner nor the drilling company were in the mining business. They were in the business of fleecing billionaires.

Still, scam or sham or simple scheme, even the exploratory drilling took a toll on the land. The shaking disrupted animals, the sound disturbed mating patterns, and the process required water to be fed into the drill at a high rate.

And water cost money.

It was also heavy. Bursum road was rated for a maximum of 7 tons per vehicle, and they were bringing in 4000 gallon tankers on the daily. At about eight pounds per gallon, it wasn't even close.

Thom began to tally the water tankers. Mr. Lester became an expert on mining permits and environmental law and reported every infraction. They recorded a documentary and got it aired on PBS. The goal was to make it as expensive as possible for the company to operate, but a little bad press never hurt either.

Or trees across the road.

Astrid and I decided to walk down the hill instead of ride in the back of the truck with the firewood. She talked about our mom, who had moved back to Maui as well. Our parents were aging. Eventually they would pass on, and we would be faced with some difficult decisions.

"Do you ever see yourself living in Mogollon?"

I couldn't deny it'd crossed my mind. But Eve was in Portland and what would I do here, build cabinets? Sell trinkets to tourists? I'd make a horrible host; I didn't know enough about the area's history or geography, not to mention its people; and you could die from loneliness, you know.

"I think I've been thinking about it wrong," I said, processing the thoughts as I spoke them. "For years there's been this part of me that figured one day, hopefully long from now, I'd have to come here to deal with Thom's stuff. Then the question might come up, would I want to stay, and I'd have to answer it then. But now I'm thinking it's the other way around. Maybe now is the best time to be here."

"I like that way of thinking."

Suddenly the week was up and it was time to take the rental car back across the desert and fly home.

"Too bad we didn't get that job," Thom said.

I agreed. "What if I come out for a month anyway? Build some stuff and see if it sells. Maybe learn a little from you."

"We could do that."

We made rough plans for a few months later and I departed, feeling good about things for once.

Chapter Thirteen: Winter 2024

On the twelfth day of Christmas my father called to me: "The job's back on," he said, "my clients finally made their design decisions. Still want to do it?"

I did. And so a few weeks later he picked me up in Albuquerque and we embarked on the trek to Mogollon once again, some thousands of dollars worth of plywood and poplar hanging out the back of his truck. It was my thirteenth trip to New Mexico and would be my twelfth time in Mogollon, and by far the longest. I was scheduled to stay for a full five weeks.

It was only the second time I'd visited in winter, the first a full twenty-nine years earlier. We were slated to get some good snow within a few days and temperatures in the teens. Thom assured me we had plenty of firewood and a space heater for the bedroom. His house's walls were sixteen inches thick, stone under plaster, and the upstairs heated fairly nicely so long as the downstairs wood stove, the one in his wood shop, was kept going. But the guest bedroom was downstairs, adjacent to the shop, and didn't receive its heat at all.

His house had been built by an Englishman named William Johns, with help from his Scottish wife's family. It was commissioned by the owner at the time, Maich Valine, after his neighbor burned down the original building in a feud. That was why the walls were stone: he'd made it fireproof.

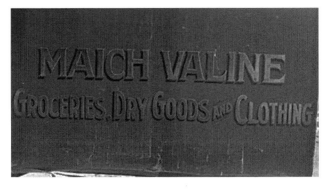

An original window blind

Some of the beams in the basement had scorch marks on them; Thom thought they were from the original building's upper structure and had been repurposed as floor joists after the fire.

Bo Mandoe

Sometime in the 1970's Hazel Maldonado had been taking a bath in the upstairs living room, probably in a metal wash basin, when some tourists walked up the front steps and peered through the glass at her. She'd had the stairs removed and Bob built a spiral staircase in the back, an amateur effort that was uneven yet fairly impressive for a beginner; it remained to this day as the primary means of getting upstairs.

Tourists still climbed the three concrete steps to the first floor porch and peered in the windows. But that was how Thom made his money.

This would be his last cabinet job. It was too much time on his feet, he told me. Too much lifting of heavy plywood and running boards through machines. He did okay with his puzzles and platters and lately he'd been making three-legged stools that people really seemed to like. So long as the road was open he didn't need to do cabinets. But it was a great opportunity to work together and teach me some things.

As we made our way up Bursum he pointed out the miners' encampment. They were still doing their exploratory drilling, moving from spot to spot within their permitted areas, drilling horizontally into the mountains as often as down. The townspeople were still hard at work resisting the operation; even Kinny had been meeting with the mining commission in Santa Fe. Mr. Lester had successfully lobbied the EPA to perform a study on the Mexican spotted owl's mating habits; this had set the company back a full two years.

We rolled slowly through town. Not much had changed on the face of it. Rusting Model-T Fords and mining carts decorated the street as always. An antique wheel had been placed atop a building in Artcher Park, cables beneath it attached to a water scoop hovering over a large well. Memorabilia from the mining days.

It struck me how ironic it was that the tourism industry played off the mining nostalgia even as its residents battled to keep the next wave out of town.

A young couple (as in, my age) had moved in to the house on the other side of the Old Kelly Store, bringing with them an eclectic sense of style that would have clashed with the mining era cabins had they not been directly across the street from the Purple Onion. They'd also bought the next building over, the general store movie set. The couple had decorated the exterior of their properties with gargoyle statues, colorful suns with faces, raven and butterfly mobiles, a full size and very ornately painted ceramic cow, a suit of armor, and the one and only stoplight in all of Catron County.

I thought of the hypnotist's yard. It was almost a relief to see such out-of-place décor in the canyon again.

We took a day to recuperate from the travel before getting down to business. By coincidence or fate the cabinets we were building were for none other than Cody McQueen, the rancher who'd picked me up hitchhiking some twenty-five years ago. There was a pleasing symmetry to it all: maybe 13 trips over 31 years *was* enough to gain a sense of the land and the people and their overlapping intentions and priorities.

"Does Dr. Kerr's wife visit often?" I asked, thinking about his water rights.

I had to repeat myself, looking straight at Thom as I spoke. He'd gotten a hearing aid but couldn't wear it in the wood shop because it filled with sawdust.

"No, it's been almost a year." A frown came over his face. "We didn't part on the greatest of terms."

"What happened?"

"You know, she's good people, Mrs. Kerr. But this was never her thing, it was the doctor's project. He really wanted to do good by the people in this town. I told you about the water. And he had all the work done putting the archive together. So the last time I saw Mrs. Kerr she said that she wanted to continue his legacy and do something good for the people here too. When I asked her what she meant, she said she was going to sell water to the miners so they didn't have to put all that wear and tear on the road getting it from the McQueens in Glenwood."

"You're kidding me."

"No, that's what she said. I think she meant well, I really do. She just hadn't thought to ask the people what *we* wanted."

"What did you tell her?"

"Oh, I said it was a horrible idea! That if she wanted to do something good for the town she'd get the miners the F- out of here!"

"And that's why you didn't part on good terms."

"Well… in the conversation it also came out that the doctor had been leasing mineral rights to the miners."

"Wait, what?"

"He'd bought up raw land outside of town too, I had no idea. I guess he had a feeling there was still gold here, so he bought the mineral rights too."

"And now he's leasing them to the miners."

"Yeah."

I thought about it for a minute. "So your well is dry and you're entirely dependent on Mrs. Kerr for your water. Which she's about to start selling to the miners, who are leasing her late husband's mineral rights, at which point she won't need your usage to keep the water rights."

A sheepish look crossed Thom's face. "After the incident I wrote a letter to Mrs. Kerr. I told her what she could do if she really wanted to help the people of Mogollon: hire someone to do the jobs Dustin Loftin used to do. Then I explained how mining leaches toxins like arsenic into the water table, and suggested what she do with her water rights: plant an orchard of fruit trees on their properties along the south-facing slope. Apples, pears, plums, and apricots all do extremely well here. It would be easy to run a water line and the mountain is already terraced! Then I signed it: water is gold."

"You didn't!"

"Hey," he said, shrugging, "sometimes people don't know until they're told."

"And then what happened?"

"Some weeks later her son showed up with a weed eater. And some months after that her daughter and husband moved to town."

"Whoa. The plot thickens."

He nodded. "I truly believe Mrs. Kerr will honor her husband's wishes."

"She never sold water to the miners, did she?"

"No," he said thoughtfully, "she did not."

#

One day Jackson Curry stopped by and dropped off a cross-eyed Siamese kitten named Silva. It'd been his daughter's cat in Arizona but she'd been unexpectedly called back to work and couldn't keep it.

The house seemed fuller with a cat somehow, more complete. Sheila and Thom pampered her like a grandchild. When we started working with power tools she curled up in a box in the corner of the wood shop and slept, but as soon as we stopped she'd come running out, mewing to be held.

Sheila was less tolerant of the noise and spent much of the time at her cabin up the street. She was spearheading a campaign to get the county to put on an official ceremony honoring Aldo Leopold on June 3rd, the date in 1924 when his efforts bore fruit and the Gila Wilderness was designated the first National Wilderness in the United States.

CALAMITY CANYON

Kinny stopped by to take us on a hike. He'd bought the house near The Tilted Windmill's original site from the neighbor he used to feud with. They'd finally come to an agreement on something, he joked. He and his girlfriend were going to open a Bed and Breakfast; it was never the wrong time for pizza.

We were well over halfway done with the job so we took the afternoon off and made the trek up the hill past the cemetery and out to Sled Saddle. He explained how the south facing slope of the canyon was gentler because it experienced a 24-hour freeze and thaw cycle in the winter, as opposed to the north facing slope which only froze and thawed maybe once a month all winter. The rapid cycling caused greater erosion and, over millennia, a gentler slope.

He pointed out the ten-inch deep ruts in the road from the water tankers. Their permits call for a cessation of all activity if they caused ruts deeper than six inches, he informed us.

He pointed out a staging area where they had a permit to disturb a fifty by fifty foot section of land. He'd walked it, he said, and it was far larger.

"A history of disregard and neglect," I said. "I'm sure you're keeping a record."

"If only I could afford a lawyer."

"If only there was a billionaire on your side."

Kinny chuckled. "Money never comes without strings."

It struck me how much time and energy – and money – it took to enforce these basic rules and regulations. And what a miracle it was that Leopold's vision had lasted this long.

If the only way to keep a company to honor its permits was for normal people like Kinny and Thom and Mr. Lester to call them out when they violated them, the only way for the Gila Wilderness to remain a wilderness was for normal people to continue to advocate for its preservation, and raise awareness when its safety was being compromised by big businesses or crony capitalists or even well-intentioned but uninformed government agencies and billionaires or their widows or heirs.

In that context Mogollon made perfect sense.

We abandoned the road for the walk home, taking an animal trail down the mountain instead. Someone had built a cairn at the spot their trail crossed the road and several further down the slope. It was easy to get lost in the mountains.

Fresh elk scat dotted the trail. "It's the time of year to find antlers," Kinny said. "You can make good money selling them."

"If you know where to look," Thom put in.

I started scanning the sides of the trail carefully. Wouldn't it be amazing to come across a set of deer or elk antlers? I'd probably keep the first one I found, if I ever did. Of course that meant we'd have to go on more hiking trips.

It had been neat to watch the weather change over the past month. From four inches of snow the first week to fifty degrees and sunshine. I'd never seen spring in

Mogollon. For the first time in my life I found myself wanting to experience a full year, see all the seasons turn.

The author's first antler

That night Thom got a call from June, their contact in Glenwood. She was calling a meeting for the next afternoon: new information had come out about the mining company and she felt it better they meet in person. Kinny and Mr. Lester had already confirmed. Thom agreed to attend, with Sheila if she was up for it.

CALAMITY CANYON

"You should come along," he told me, "you'd like June. She's an interesting character."

As underwhelming of an adjective as interesting might be, especially in a place entirely populated, one could say saturated, with intriguing and unique characters, June Bethesda took the prize. On a scant half-acre lot in the middle of Glenwood's tiny suburban district she'd managed to cram a working mini-ranch with two horses, geese, chickens, dogs, pigs, and even a donkey. In and around this free-range grazing area she'd constructed several tiny houses, each of whose history she explained in great detail before starting the meeting.

There was a two-story water tower sculpture made from salvaged mining equipment and part of the original Catwalk bridge the Forest Service had given her after the flood.

A fire pit area was decorated with ten foot long drill bit extensions bent into gentle curves, sprouting from the ground and reaching outwards.

"I like how you've altered the material," I told her. "It's not just rusting junk sitting by the road anymore."

An outhouse sported a mule motif. *This is where you put your ass.*

One of the tiny houses was an eight by ten foot stone and concrete bunker which had originally been a cistern. There was an elaborate aqueduct to feed water to the entire, once much larger, ranch. But they'd used sand from the creek to mix the cement and it didn't hold water, June told us. She'd had a doorway cut into the side and used it to keep things out now.

"I'm giving myself twenty-five years to find someone to take this over," she explained, all five feet of solid muscle working as she opened the oaken door. "That's how long I figure I've got left. People ask me, why are you collecting all this stuff? Someone's just gonna have to get rid of it. But not if I find the right person!"

We sat on familiar looking stools in the bunker, all six of us: June, Thom, Sheila, Kinny, Mr. Lester, and myself. It had come to light that the permits issued to the mining company had come from a bureau that didn't have jurisdiction below the level of the ground. At the recent meeting in Santa Fe Kinny pointed this out to the mining commission, and after the meeting several of the board members had come up to him privately and informed him that he had grounds to sue the bureau.

"Wasn't this just a technicality?" I wanted to know.

"Yes, of course," Kinny said, "but while it got sorted out we could have their permits declared void and the miners would have to stop operations. It would cost them money, which is the whole goal. These companies only speak one language."

"I still think we should petition to get the graveyard declared an historic site," June said. "Then they couldn't tear up the road anymore."

"Right," Mr. Lester scoffed, "because this country always honors and respects graveyards."

"As long as they're white people!" Sheila clarified, missing his sarcasm.

"While we're at it, why not petition to turn the town into a National Monument?" Kinny said. "It would help the economy."

"And ruin the ecology!" Mr. Lester snapped. "That many people? There goes the neighborhood. It would be worse than the miners."

"People have to make a living somehow," June pointed out. "They can't all work remotely."

Mr. Lester winced. He worked for a systems solutions outfit based out of Socorro. Forty years ago they'd been tasked with studying the gray wolf population in the Gila Wilderness. He'd bought his house during the job and never left, working by phone and then by modem and eventually online. He'd been the first person in Catron County with a Starlink.

"It doesn't matter," said Thom, speaking for the first time. "Have you been to a National Monument? Every one of them has huge parking lots and room for tour buses to turn around. They have public bathrooms. Infrastructure. We don't have that and I don't think any of us want it."

No, everyone agreed, they didn't want that.

Nothing was settled during the meeting. They went around and around, more a voicing of complaints than a seeking of solutions. Was tourism an extractive industry? Was mining softer on the landscape? Could the town survive without either? Could the land survive humanity without human intervention?

We drove home silently, Thom and Sheila in the front and me cramped in the back of the extra cab. I'd be leaving in a few days, back to civilization and the real world, whatever that meant. Because it wasn't really any different out there, just more people and more complex issues to deal with. Overlapping priorities and beliefs and ways of going about their business.

Mogollon wasn't unique in its history of scams and shams and feuds and infighting. It was a fractal example of the greater society in the same way that the general store movie set from 1973 was an historic marker. The town was a reflection of itself, just as the United States of America as it existed in this moment in time was a reflection of who its people had become. One could look at the general store and feel the nostalgia for the Gold Rush era even though the store didn't exist then, just as one could conjure up the dream of this country's forefathers and never question whether there was any further truth, any other story to be told, any counter perspective worth considering.

This was the value of the eclectic art in and around Mogollon: it caused you to question the reality of what you were seeing. A track of mining carts along the roadside told a certain tale. It fit in with the narrative of the ghost town and the wild west and the glorification of the gold rush. But a suit of armor? A painted cow? A two-story water tower art sculpture? At some point you had to wonder if there was something more to the story.

A dozen Department of Transportation trucks huddled on the mesa as we drove past. Thom slowed down and one of the workers ambled over.

"We're gonna be doing some work next week," he said, "it'll be one lane for a while. Maybe closed now and then."

"Ah, okay… my son flies out on Wednesday," Thom said, "will we be able to get out?"

The man shrugged.

"What are you guys doing?"

"Standard maintenance."

Bursum road

We drove on. The road did need maintenance. Several spots along the edge were fraying, chunks of asphalt falling into the drainage ditch or down the slope itself. At the sheerest part of the cliff, where iron stakes had been driven into the mountain to hold up sheet metal supports for the road, the pavement had visibly cracked. White spray paint lines attested to the DOT's plans.

Further up the mountain we met a string of water tankers coming down. We pulled over to let them pass, Thom raising a hand in greeting to each driver.

"Why are you waving?" Sheila sniffed.

"They're just workers," Thom said, "I don't have anything against them."

Personally, I loved Catron County's tradition of waving at passing cars on the roadways. In a large, rural county of 3700 people it was still somewhat of an occasion. Sometimes it was enough to tilt the tip of your hand off the steering wheel in acknowledgment. Whether miners, ranchers, hippies or otherwise, it was nice to know your neighbors would lift a finger for you.

And not always the middle one.

After the tankers passed, the rear pilot truck stopped to chat. "We're pulling out," said the driver, "it's mating season."

"That's interesting," said Thom. "They're about to start road construction."

"Isn't road construction loud?" Sheila said, belaboring the obvious.

The miner's face reddened. "I have to do what I'm told," he said. "They said to pull everything out like we weren't coming back, and if anyone asked to blame it on the spotted owl. You guys have always been respectful even though we know you don't want us here. Thought I'd return the favor."

#

We finished the job without incident and still had time to go antler hunting; both Thom and I found a Coos deer antler, a left and a right though not matching and from different years. A late storm brought a dusting of snow and muddy roads above town. We stoked the fire in the woodshop and settled down to play a game of cribbage.

Tourists drove by at frequent intervals. "Must be spring," Thom said, "I'll have to start making puzzles soon."

"This was your last cabinet job. How does it feel to be retired?"

"Oh, you're never really retired out here. Still have to garden and gather firewood for the winter. The puzzles pay the bills though. It's a good life."

I had to agree.

A man walked up the front steps and peered through the door's hundred year old paned glass window.

"Tourist," said Thom, "maybe you'd better get this."

I went to the door with a feeling of pride: I was the woodworker's son, walking in his footsteps, and even if I couldn't represent the entire history of this town there was no doubt I was participating in this moment of it.

"Hi, said the man at the door, a well-tanned businessman in a tailored suit. "I'm in town on behalf of a family member who's selling the old Crenshaw cabin up the road. Do you know any carpenters who might be interested in a project?"

The End

Afterword

This book is based on true events. While it is fiction, many of the incidents did happen to somebody in Mogollon at some point in time, allegedly. Names and dates have been changed for privacy but the historical information in particular is verifiably accurate.

And yet that history spans such a brief period of time! From James Cooney's first discovery of gold in 1870 to the company town's dismantling around 1942: so much focus on such a short window.

Sometime around the 1980s a company leased land outside of Mogollon from the Forest Service to run a high-tech smelting operation, going through old mine tailings with improved techniques to leach out even more minerals, though with no less toxic byproducts. That effort did not last long, however, and the equipment has been abandoned: more public land fenced off and declared a biohazard.

This is the pattern of extractive capitalism and the danger of a short term history: there is nothing standing in the way of these companies retreading the process over and over in the pristine forests and wildernesses that still grace this planet.

Nothing but you and me, that is.

I wrote this book to provide a fuller sense of the issues and events that the people of Mogollon, and in a way much of the United States of America, are facing today. Are the only options to revert to who we used to be or to make a living off the nostalgia for that time? How does a normal person get their foot in the door when 99% of an industry – or a town – is already owned by billionaires or corporations? When the line between scam and scheme depends on how much you can spend on lawyers?

Conservation is not a value that trickles down. To preserve what wilderness remains, it will have to transpirate up from the grassroots to reach every branch and leaf of the human tree.

Acknowledgements

This book would not exist without the encouragement and support of my online community. Special shouts out to Carol Morgan, Ty Gill, Tamlyn Overmier, Bethany Armstrong, Jennifer Armerding, and Frank Munden. Big thanks to Bonnie and Niels Mandoe for setting great examples by growing into yourselves. Thanks to Stan King for the hikes. Thanks to Marianne Scharn for caring. Thanks to Prana and Niels for reading the first draft.

A special acknowledgement to H.A. Hoover's *Tales from the Bloated Goat: Early Days in Mogollon*. Anyone interested in reading about the town's heyday would do well to find a copy.

Also worth reading: *Hypnotizing Chickens and other stories* by Jan Sherman, a firsthand account of growing up in Mogollon as a young child.

Respect to John Steinbeck for inspiration found within *The Pastures of Heaven*.

A polite lift of a finger to the people of Catron County. May you reach your destination safely.

A cup of tea for the Danes.

And finally, hats off to Aldo Leopold. May your vision never waver in the hearts and minds of the dwellers of this land.

Made in the USA
Middletown, DE
04 February 2025